OTHER PLACES

OTHER PLACES

A Story Collection

By

THOMAS SMITH

CEMETERY DANCE PUBLICATIONS

Baltimore

2024

Other Places

Trade Paperback Edition

ISBN:
978-1-58767-978-0

Cemetery Dance Publications
132B Industry Lane, Unit #7
Forest Hill, MD 21050
www.cemeterydance.com

Contents

For Joe Cherkes.
Friend, confidant, and all-around good egg

And always for Melanie for a thousand and one reasons

Take heed you find not, that you do not seek.

—6th Century English Proverb

Go then, there are other worlds than these.

—Stephen King, *The Dark Tower: The Gunslinger*

It's a beautiful, terrible world, isn't it?

—Dean Koontz, *The Silent Corner*

Presto

Lawrence Valentine took a deep breath, closed his eyes, and levitated.

Just a few inches at first. Just high enough for them to see that he was off the ground. Then he held his position and counted to himself.

One...two...three...four...five...six...seven.

For some reason seven seemed to be the magic number. By the end of a slow count to seven the people who had come to be amazed were well on their way, and those who came to nudge the person closest to them and say, *"That ain't no big deal. I seen David Blaine do it. And I know how it's done..."* had their elbows working and their smug self-satisfied expressions planted firmly on their faces.

Then the magician made their jaws drop.

He rose another few inches in the air and began to float. Eight inches above the stage, then eight inches above the heads of the audience. He floated above them, stopping over random members of the audience long enough for them to see that there were no wires, no harnesses.

Long enough to stop the know-it-alls in mid-sentence.

Long enough to see his wife and his doctor were missing.

Again.

After a few moments he came down in the far right-hand aisle and jogged to the front of the stage. Then he levitated back to his original spot.

The applause was overwhelming, but it was wasted on him. His mind was elsewhere. It was only after an assistant crossed over and, in a sweeping flourish, nudged him and whispered, "*Lawrence, go say something*," that he moved toward the front of the stage and acknowledged the audience.

"Ladies and gentlemen," he said as the noise finally subsided to a manageable level, "that would normally be the end of the show. But since this is my last night with you until next year's tour, I would like to offer one last mystery for your consideration." He gestured to the crew in the light booth. "Would you bring the house lights up please?" When the theater was completely illuminated, he continued.

"In preparing for this evening's performance I made a request of the theater manager. I asked him to select twenty-five numbers at random. Any twenty-five numbers between one and two thousand. Then I made what may have been an odd request."

Lawrence Valentine stood at the edge of the stage and looked out across the theater. His fifth sold out show of the week, the last show of the run. And tonight, he was going to do something no magician had ever done before. Not Blackstone, not Houdini, not Ching Ling Soo, not even David Copperfield or Lance Burton.

Tonight, he would not only create the ultimate magic effect.

He would create pandemonium.

"Three months ago, I called this theater and asked the manager to make all of the preparations for this final mystery. I told him what I would need, provided the necessary funds through my agent, and have had no further contact with him since that phone call. This morning I was assured that he has made the arrangements as requested." Lawrence watched as every eye locked on him. Almost every face looked up at him with something just short of reverence. This audience was his and they would follow him anywhere. Believe anything.

Tonight, they would believe in magic.

"That being said," he continued, "I would like to ask Malcom Barnwell, the manager of the Grand Avenue Theater, to join me." A dapper Englishman stepped out of the wings and approached from stage right to polite applause. Tall, elegant, and dressed in a Savile Row suit, Lawrence could not have asked for a better assistant.

The two men shook hands and Lawrence continued. "As Mr. Barnwell explains the arrangements he has made, members of his staff will be rolling out a sheet of heavy three-inch-thick rubber. Please understand, it has absolutely nothing to do with what is about to happen other than to protect the stage floor." He gestured toward the manager. "Mr. Barnwell."

The Englishman cleared his throat and began. "Approximately three months ago, well after the contract for this week of performances had been signed, Mr. Valentine called and asked me to make certain preparations for this evening. At that time, he was adamant that there be no further communication between us considering those particular requests. I have communicated with his road manager about routine aspects of the show, such as when his trucks should arrive, how many people will require hotel rooms, and the normal logistical aspects of making any large production possible. But Mr. Valentine and I have not had communication of any kind since he phoned me." He smiled and turned toward the magician. "Though I must admit, I am intrigued by your requests. It sounds as if you are planning to build a bomb shelter on the premises."

The audience laughed, as did everyone onstage. The rubber sheet was now in place and the manager's staff was standing by.

"That's an intriguing idea," the magician said, "and if I ever develop an illusion which utilizes a makeshift bomb shelter, I will make sure my agent sends you a royalty check." After the resulting titter subsided, Lawrence Valentine continued. "But as for the matter at hand, do you have the list of random numbers I requested during our phone call?"

The manager removed an envelope from his inside coat pocket and held it up.

"Very good," the magician continued. "There are two thousand seats in the theater, and each seat bears a number on a small brass plate on the left arm. I am now going to ask Mr. Barnwell to read the list of twenty-five random numbers he selected. If you are occupying a seat that corresponds to a number he calls out, please come to the stage."

Music flowed from the hidden speakers and twenty-five pleasantly surprised people made their way to the stage as their numbers were called. After he greeted each one, Lawrence Valentine addressed the manager again. "Mr. Barnwell, what was my next request?"

"You requested that I contact whatever metalworkers I thought appropriate and have them construct an iron box six and a half feet tall, four feet wide, and four feet deep. They were to weld every piece of the box together except the front panel. Then, they were to deliver it here tonight."

"And has that been done?"

"Yes. The box is just offstage and the gentlemen who constructed it are awaiting your instructions."

"In that case," Lawrence said, turning on his heel and making a sweeping gesture, "bring out the box."

An engine roared to life offstage and a few seconds later a forklift rolled across the rubber sheet and stopped when Lawrence Valentine raised his hand. A dull grayish-chrome box rested on the forks, complete except for the front panel. The forklift driver lowered the box and the three men tilted it far enough for the driver to pull the forks out and return to his spot offstage. The men, each wearing caps and coveralls, lowered the side of the box to the stage and stepped back.

Lawrence Valentine saluted the men and turned back to the audience. "Ladies and gentlemen, this is exactly what I requested. Now I have just one question." He looked at the manager. "What is it?"

The audience laughed and the theater manager looked flustered for a second. Then he caught the joke. "This, Mr. Valentine, is a metal box. Built to your specifications. No gaps. Completely constructed and welded to be airtight and watertight by the gentlemen I selected after a few days of careful research."

"And who are those gentlemen?"

"They are members of the local ironworkers union."

As the audience applauded, the magician thanked the men and remarked on the solid construction job. Then he asked what they used to construct the box.

"The box is constructed from one-inch carbon steel panels," said one of the men. "There is one more panel that will fit here in the front, and as we were instructed, we drilled three one-inch holes into the top of the panel."

"That's perfect," Lawrence said. "Please get the panel and I'll explain what we are going to do." Two men went offstage and retrieved the last panel as Lawrence Valentine walked over and stood in front of the iron box. "Now that all the pieces are here, let's assemble them. Mr. Barnwell, would you please have the twenty-five volunteers make a human circle around the box. Space them out so these men can finish the job.

As the manager brought the audience members to the stage, Lawrence turned his attention back to the audience. "Now, while he is positioning the volunteers, I would like to ask the gentlemen who built the box to do one more thing." He turned to face the workmen. "Gentlemen, would you please weld the panel onto the front of the box?"

The men brought out two welding units and positioned one on each side of the box. When the first unit went live, Lawrence Valentine said, "Wait. I forgot one thing." He stepped into the box. "This will be a lot more impressive if I'm in here. You see, that's what the three holes are for." He motioned to the last panel. "I'm very fond of breathing. Now, gentlemen, weld the last panel in place, hit the box three times with a hammer when you're finished, then stand back."

Nobody moved.

"Mr. Valentine," said the ironworker closest to him, "once we weld that panel, you won't be able to get out. You'll be sealed in there permanently."

"Don't bet on it," Lawrence said as he tossed his microphone to an assistant and stepped to the back of the box. The ironworkers shrugged, then fitted the final panel in place. One man braced it while the other two welded. It took ten minutes to weld the panel, but the audience didn't seem to notice. They watched in various combinations of amusement, bewilderment, and horror as the box was sealed shut. Then one of the men hit the box three times with a hammer and they moved out of the circle.

There was no music.

There were no whirling laser effects to distract the audience.

There was only the iron box surrounded by twenty-five volunteers, three nervous welders, and a theater manager who tried to maintain a sense of dignity and decorum, while simultaneously wringing his hands.

They watched the box.

One minute.

Three.

Seven.

Eleven minutes and forty-five seconds.

Someone in the audience started crying. Then one of the volunteers gasped.

While the front panel had shown no outward sign of change, an outline slowly materialized. Faint. Soft and grainy. Indistinct. Then it took on a form.

The form of a man.

In the next two minutes the form became more distinct, though it seemed to be surrounded by a sort of haze. Like watching someone move through a layer of gauze. Then, as if he had originally been part of the metal itself, Lawrence Valentine seemed to pull away from the face of the front panel. He lurched forward and stepped onto the stage floor in front of the box.

There was silence for almost ten seconds.

One of the welders fainted.

Then the audience erupted.

They leaped to their feet and the resulting cacophony was beyond deafening. The cheers, applause, stomping, crying, and screams pounded the stage like a sonic tidal wave. The floor of the stage vibrated with the sheer force of the frenzied applause. Hundreds of people were crying openly, and in addition to the welder, sixty audience members also passed out.

The ovation lasted seventeen minutes.

At some point an assistant brought a chair out for Lawrence. He sat down heavily, and before his assistant could move, he gripped her arm and asked, "Where is Angela?"

The assistant stared at him, finally finding her voice. "I think she had another migraine. The doctor went back to check on her just after the show started."

Lawrence nodded, released her, and massaged his temples with both hands. After a few minutes he stood and walked to the front of the stage, the applause still deafening, and motioned for quiet.

"A car vanishes. Beautiful assistants are transported from the stage to the balcony and back. A man floats on air and seemingly walks through solid steel. This is my world, and I thank you for being a part of it this evening. Tonight, I have shown you mystery and you have in turn allowed me into your hearts. And is that not, after all, what life is all about? Thank you and goodnight."

The audience roared its approval again as the curtain closed. The magician went back to the chair and sat. No one spoke for half a minute, then the manager said, "Mister Valentine, do you want to go back out for another bow?" There was uncertainty in his voice. Uncertainty and awe.

Lawrence looked up and shook his head. "I'm afraid that last effect took a lot out of me. I'm not even sure I can stand for more than a minute or two right now."

"Oh certainly," the manager said. "Certainly. I can only imagine. And may I say that was…it was just…I mean," the manager stopped and closed his eyes as if in a kind of rapture, "there are no words."

"Thank you. You're very kind," Lawrence said. "But with your permission, I think I'm going back to the dressing room to rest while the crew tears the set down."

"Oh absolutely. And again, that was the most magnificent thing I have ever seen."

Lawrence smiled at the manager's words as an assistant helped him to a waiting trailer.

•

"Have you lost your mind?" asked Dr. Harry Cryder as he parted Lawrence's black shoulder-length hair and located the port. "Whatever you did out there was just a step away from suicide. Just what the hell were you thinking? And more than that, why didn't you tell anybody that you planned to do some new illusion with the potential to tax your system like this? I mean, what the hell did you *do* out there?"

Lawrence sat still while the doctor worked behind him. Of the four trailers that traveled with the show, one was the domain of Dr. Harry Cryder. It looked like a combination medical facility and electronic engineer's playground. All designed by Dr. Harry Cryder to monitor and treat Lawrence should the need arise.

"I told you last night I was working on something revolutionary. Something unlike anything that's ever been done before," Lawrence said. "As for what it is, it's too bad you missed it. I'm amazed that the sheer noise level of the audience's response didn't bring you running." He looked at the doctor for a long moment, looking for some small tell, and then continued. "Besides, I didn't want to waste time talking about me when you and my wife were missing during most of the show. According to Katrina, Angela had another one of her headaches. So how is she now?"

Harry's eyes narrowed a fraction. "Your wife is fine," he said. "Fortunately, we caught the migraine before it had the chance to become a full-blown event again. But this one was so bad I had to give her an injection of Sumatriptan, and when I left she was sleeping."

"Well that certainly *was* fortunate," Lawrence said, not bothering to look at the doctor.

"Yes it was, but let's not change the subject," Harry said as he connected a probe to the port at the base of Lawrence's skull and turned to the bank of equipment on his right. "What you're really saying is that you knew whatever you were going to do was both dangerous and stupid but you did it anyway. Is that pretty much the gist of it?" He made two quick adjustments and watched a small screen where two lines intersected then formed perfect parallel lines.

"In case you've forgotten, you were almost killed when that car jumped the sidewalk and hit you in New York two years ago. And the only reason you can even move today is the experimental artificial tissue that has been grafted onto the existing undamaged tissue along your spine."

"Yes, the so-called cyborg tissue. I know, I know. And it works like a charm." He shifted to better see the doctor from the corner of his eye. "It works even better than we imagined."

"Even so," the doctor said, "the tissue is still in the experimental stage. The world's top researchers in physics, chemistry, biology, mathematics, and engineering still don't know what this stuff can do. It was originally developed for mechanical and electronic uses. So how it affects humans is still a complete unknown."

The doctor stood in front of Lawrence and shook his head. "Lawrence, that tissue is structured with carbon nanotubes and fungal cells derived from a specific caterpillar fungus, because the cordycepin which is derived from the fungus has amazing anti-inflammatory properties."

"To which I am a living testament," Lawrence said as he spread his hands and took a small bow.

"True. But it also has properties we know nothing about, and until we know exactly what we're dealing with, we can't be too careful." The doctor replaced the small flap of skin and walked back to the monitor.

"That's why you picked the wrong time to miss a performance. The audience saw something that changed their view of magic. And if they knew for a fact that it wasn't some kind of illusion—that it was the real thing—it would change their lives. Maybe even shatter a few."

The doctor replaced the small flap of skin and walked in front of Lawrence. "Even so, you have to be careful." He took the magician's wrist and timed his pulse.

"Oh, I'm being careful. I—" The words died in his throat when the images came. First in ones and twos, then a tidal wave of sight and sound. Nothing clear. Just images, hazy around the edges like old Polaroid photos. But the subject was clear.

The two of them.

Harry and Angela.

Together.

Lawrence pulled away, and as he broke contact with the doctor, the images, cries, and guttural sounds of passion faded into the darkness. He stared into the distance, struggling to regain his focus.

"Lawrence, what's wrong? Talk to me Lawrence. What's going on with you?" The doctor took a step forward, but the magician waved him off.

"You know something," Lawrence said, "you walked into that operating room and grafted a total of two feet of this cyborg tissue onto my existing tissue without knowing exactly what it would do. Two feet of tissue complete with little nanobots to do the parts of the surgery you couldn't do by hand. All the time *hoping* it might help me walk again."

"And the gamble paid off," the doctor said, his voice sharp.

"Oh yes, it paid off alright," Lawrence said. He stood and moved his head from side to side, working his shoulder muscles. "In fact, it paid off in spades. Because of your little experiment, I can manipulate objects near me. I can levitate," he said, making parenthetical motions in the air, "by creating a solid cushion of air between me and the floor. Or any other solid object, like the heads of the people in the audience."

The doctor looked at him, mouth open. Lawrence chuckled, shook his head, and continued.

"And just tonight I discovered a new ability. One that is going to drive a wedge between you and my wife." His eyes went dark. "Break it off Harry. Now. Tonight."

The doctor blinked. "What are you talking about?"

"Don't insult my intelligence. All I'm going to say is it ends tonight. Either you tell her or I will." He threw the door open with enough force to dent the sheet metal when the door knob struck the inner wall, and walked out into the night. Harry watched from the doorway, stunned and confused.

And frightened.

•

"Lawrence, that effect you performed two weeks ago still has the magic world talking. Even David Copperfield has said it is the single most amazing thing he has ever seen. And I never thought anyone would top his flying illusion."

"Well, that is high praise indeed," Lawrence said to the portly gentleman who had corralled him into a corner and seemed intent on keeping him there. It was the very reason he hated meeting with his investors. The party was always nice. Always held in a home that cost more than a city block in Kansas. But there was always someone who wanted to monopolize his time. A combination of being star struck and feeling just a little entitled. Still, these were the people who made the show possible, and most of them were relatively nice people who meant well. And since he had become a major headliner, they didn't try to tell him what to do with their money. So it could have been worse. Even the constant buzzing he had been hearing since his meeting with the doctor wasn't a major distraction.

Unlike a case of tinnitus, it wasn't debilitating or annoying. But it was insistent. As if someone was trying to whisper a vital secret to him.

Someone or something.

"There you are, Lawrence." He felt a hand on his shoulder as the hostess came to rescue him. "I thought Richard might have cornered you so he could pick your brain. He fancies himself something of an amateur magician."

Lawrence turned to his host and smiled, hoping the relief didn't show on his face. "As a matter of fact, Mr. Bennington and I were just talking shop. That's what happens when you put two magicians together. The topic of conversation ultimately turns to magic and the latest effects." He turned back to his rotund benefactor. "Mr. Bennington you'll have to come to the shop one afternoon and I'll show you where the magic is created."

The portly grocery baron beamed. "I certainly will. Thank you very much. But please, just one more question. Magician to magician. How did you do the iron box effect?"

Lawrence smiled. "I just walked through the front of the box. Just walked through solid steel like it was water."

Richard Bennington looked stunned for a moment, then he placed his index finger alongside his nose and grinned. "I get it. A magician never tells his secrets."

Lawrence winked, mimicked the gesture, and allowed himself to be led off by his hostess. Margaret Thorson steered Lawrence away from the beaming grocery tycoon. "Oh, you've done it now," she said. "For the next month he'll be telling everyone he knows that he has been invited to your workshop to see the inner workings of your enterprise."

He glanced back and watched as Richard Bennington gripped the elbow of another guest and began gesturing toward them and talking non-stop. "He's a nice enough man," Lawrence said. "He's just a little, ah, exuberant."

"Well, I'm afraid you might find me a little exuberant as well," she said, "because I have something I can't wait to show you." They walked down a long hallway and entered the library.

The room was a combination of walnut, brass, leather furniture, knick-knacks that would have been at home in any museum, and an underlying hint of Blackwoods Flake Personal Reserve pipe tobacco. The majority of the books were bound in leather, easily cost anywhere from a few hundred to a few thousand dollars each, and unlike other such books in home libraries he had visited, many of these showed signs of having actually been read.

Margaret released his arm and walked over to a large painting and swung the picture on a set of hidden hinges to reveal a wall safe. "I know this whole safe behind the picture frame thing is a bit of a cliché, but my husband Harold likes it. He says it reminds him of something out of a James Bond film." Margaret manipulated the dial and opened the safe. She removed an object and brought it to him.

"Harold bought this for me at an auction a few weeks ago," she said as she handed him an antique fountain pen. "It is supposed to have belonged to Houdini, but I am never sure about these things. Do you know someone who could authenticate it for us?"

Lawrence looked at the pen and thought for a moment. "Actually, you should take this to Denis Behr. He is one of the world's leading magic scholars. If he can't authenticate it, he will probably know who can. Call me tomorrow and I'll give you his manager's number, and then I'll let them know to expect your call." He handed the pen back to her and watched as she replaced it and locked the safe. He wondered for a brief moment if they would miss one of the bricks of hundreds or other valuables that shared space with the pen.

As they left the library, Margaret said, "I'm sorry your wife couldn't be here tonight. Is she not feeling well?" The magician shook his head. "No, she hasn't been feeling well for the last few weeks. She has developed migraines recently, so she has been staying in for the most part."

"Oh Lawrence, I'm so sorry to hear that," she said as she took his arm and walked with him toward the door. "But as I understand it, since the accident you've had a doctor who travels with your troupe. Has he been able to do anything for her?"

"Oh yes," Lawrence said, his smile less than sincere. "He's been very attentive."

•

Lawrence left the house in Waterbury, Connecticut earlier than he had planned and drove to the Gotham Hotel on 46th Street in New York. That's where the cast and crew was staying in preparation for a small show and lecture at Berkeley College the next evening. The original plan had been for him to stay with his hosts and leave the next morning, but he used his wife's illness as an excuse to go back early.

His visit with the doctor and subsequent conversation with Margaret had sealed the deal, and the hour and forty-five-minute drive had given him time to think. And a man who could pass through solid objects had a lot of options to think about.

Lawrence pulled up to the hotel a few minutes after midnight. The parking attendant took the keys to the rental car, and Lawrence Valentine went up to his room. It was empty. It was what he expected, but not what he had hoped. There was always the outside chance that Angela really had developed migraines. It happened.

But probably not this time.

He took the elevator down to Harry's room. The sounds coming from inside were unmistakable. There was groaning coming from the other side of the door, but not the kind associated with migraines or any other illness. These were not sounds of pain.

They were the sounds of confirmation.

He knew the door was locked, but that would pose no problem. He put his hands against the hotel room door and took a deep breath. His spine tingled slightly, just like it always did when he tapped into that part of himself. All he needed to do was fix the desired result in his mind and relax. The tissue and the lovely little nanobots would take care of the rest.

He slowed his breathing, closed his eyes, and reached out. He felt his hand merge with the door.

Then he pulled back.

He had a better idea.

Lawrence walked down the hall and around a corner. He took out his cell phone and called Harry's room. Just before the voicemail kicked in, the doctor answered. He sounded distracted.

"Hello. Lawrence? Do you know what time it is?" There was a slight pause, then the doctor's voice took on an edge. "Don't tell me you're calling to check up on me after your tirade the other night."

"Harry, I know it's late and I'm sorry if I disturbed you. The fact is I was supposed to be away until tomorrow, but earlier tonight I started having some shooting pains along my spine. Like little daggers slicing me up and down. And since it's never happened before I should probably come back and have you take a look. But if I'm causing you a problem of some kind…"

"Oh hey, Lawrence, no. You did the right thing," the doctor said, his tone mellowing immediately. "Now tell me again what happened."

"Like I said, it started tonight and I've never felt anything like this before. It's like a hundred little knives stabbing me at once."

The doctor asked more questions and Lawrence supplied what he thought were feasible answers. Then Harry began running through possible scenarios of what the issues might be. Lawrence listened to the monologue and smiled. A cold empty gesture that didn't reach his eyes.

The doctor asked if he was near, and the reptilian smile widened.

"Yeah," he said, "I'm about fifteen minutes away. Can you meet me at the medical trailer?"

He listened another moment and put the phone back in his pocket.

Three minutes later his wife left the room and hurried down the opposite hall toward the elevator. When the doors closed and he was sure she was gone, Lawrence walked over and knocked on the doctor's door.

"Did you forget...?" Harry opened the door and stopped abruptly, his eyes wide.

"Did I forget what?" Lawrence watched as the doctor struggled to regain his composure. He pushed his way past the doctor and stood by the bed. "From the looks of things, you must have been pretty restless," he said, pointing to the tangled sheets. "Either that, or you had company." He crossed his arms and watched the doctor.

"Company? What company would I have had?" he asked as he closed the door. "I'm not seeing anyone right now."

"Oh, I'm not so sure about that," the magician said. "I'm almost certain that was my wife I saw leaving a few minutes ago. And she looked more than a little disheveled." He closed his eyes. "My guess is you saw a lot of her."

"Lawrence, I don't know what you're talking about."

"Harry, please. I'm not stupid. So don't make things worse by lying to me. I saw what you two were doing.

"All of it."

The doctor's face blanched. Everything Lawrence Valentine needed to know was in that expression. Then the expression changed.

"Do you mean to tell me you were watching us?" The doctor put a hand to his face and looked around the room. "Were you in here just a few minutes ago?

"No, but I could hear you though the door. And I told you two weeks ago you should break it off." He held his hands out palm up and shook his head. "Why, Harry? What were you thinking?"

The doctor faltered for a moment, then seemed to gain strength. He stood straight. "Why? Because you have been spending more time working on your precious magic show than attending to your wife. You lock yourself away for days at a time doing whatever it is you're doing. You don't see anybody. Don't talk to anybody. And no woman wants to be neglected that way."

"So since you both thought I've been so inattentive, and instead of approaching me directly and making your case, you somehow decided screwing each other's brains out was the best solution? You really thought that was the best way to make your point?"

"We couldn't talk to you. You were always locked away in the warehouse doing God only knows what."

"You know what I was doing. Like I told you before, I was making us all rich beyond our wildest dreams. Damn it Harry, I have the ability to make everybody from Houdini to David Copperfield look like amateurs working a kid's birthday party. I can do things nobody else on the *planet* can do. And it's all because of the procedure you performed after I was hit by that car.

"The thing is, the little nanobots didn't stop their construction once the tissue graft was complete. Oh no. After that little job was finished, they began to synthesize the cordycepin. And once they did that, some interesting things began to happen. And in the end, you changed me. Made me into something new." Lawrence walked toward the doctor, and just as he suspected, the doctor backed up until his back was against the door.

The thing that had once been Lawrence moved to within inches of him and glared. He could smell the doctor's sweat. Could smell the fear.

He inched closer, leaned in, and whispered in the doctor's ear.

You turned me into a god.

Without looking he motioned toward the open pocket door that separated the sleeping area from the sitting area and it slammed shut. He motioned toward the mirror over the vanity in the dressing area and it shattered, the web of fractured glass dividing their reflection into thousands of realities. Lawrence registered the shock on the doctor's face. "And that means, dear doctor, that I know what you and my wife have been up to." His eyes flashed and his lips drew back into a snarl. "I know about the convenient migraines during the shows and the not-so-secret trysts you two had while I was working my ass off for you and everyone else in this company."

"Lawrence, look. I'm sorry," Harry said, his face a mask of white. "We didn't expect it to happen. We just..."

"Harry, shut up," Lawrence said, an expression of calm replacing the one of rage. "It's not like I had to have some special powers to figure it out. Everybody knew about it. And a few of the more loyal members of the company even tried to make me aware, though I had a hard time believing it at first." He stopped, crossed his left arm across his stomach, and rested his right elbow on his left wrist. Cradled his chin in his right hand. "But Harry, what's done is done. So instead of getting mad, I'm going to do what I came here to do." He opened his arms wide.

The doctor flinched.

"I'm going to show you the new trick."

Lawrence took another step forward, made contact.

And kept moving forward.

Harry Cryder made a wet, choking sound. He bucked and tried to pull away from the door, but that only caused him to merge with the oncoming magician that much faster. He opened his mouth to scream, but all that came out was a thin reedy hiss.

For a moment Harry and Lawrence looked like something out of an H. P. Lovecraft nightmare. Something that had once been two men and was now an abomination of tangled limbs and heads. A nightmare beast from some nether realm, or one of the elder gods awakening.

For a moment there was the hellish conglomeration.

Then, there was only a distended version of Harry.

•

Harry Cryder took a step away from the door, stumbled, and fell. He felt an immense pressure building inside him. His skin felt too tight. Felt like it was going to split. For a brief moment he saw the image of a sausage sizzling on the grill, the casing splitting. He crawled along the floor to the canopy bed, grabbed one of the four posts, and tried to haul himself up. His hand slipped. He wasn't in control of his body any more. He felt like he was being manipulated by some unseen force.

Then realization dawned like a sunrise in hell.

A split second before Lawrence Valentine solidified inside his body, Harry clutched the bedpost and heard a single word.

Presto.

Then he was ripped apart.

•

Twenty minutes later, Lawrence Valentine opened the door to his room and walked in. A small chunk of brain matter fell from his lapel. His wife was just coming out of the adjoining sitting room.

"Oh Lawrence, I didn't expect you back tonight."

"I know you didn't," he said as she stopped abruptly. "But I'm glad you're up." He moved toward her and opened his arms wide. "I have something new to show you."

The Heart is a Determined Hunter

The moment Lloyd McPherson dialed the telephone the world went dark. At least that was the illusion created by the first dark clouds of the coming storm as they pushed the October sun out of the way. As it was, Lloyd barely noticed. His connection had already failed twice, and the one that was coaxing the second ring from the phone on the other end was tenuous at best.

He had debated the idea of calling the Steadman Resort for almost two days and, right or wrong, he had finally placed the call. The line popped and crackled; the ghosts of past conversations unaware they were long finished. Lloyd's finger hovered over the tiny plunger that held the power to terminate the connection. Twice he had pulled back at the last second. Scant seconds from the comforting buzz of a new dial tone. He was still not too sure.

"Thank you for calling the Steadman Resort. How may I be of service this afternoon?"

"What?" The world swam back into focus in one large wave. "Oh...yes, I'm sorry. I was a little preoccupied."

"Of course, sir. How may I be of service?" The voice was steady. That sort of well bred, professionally aloof hotel voice. A voice that implied the sort of patience gained after a lifetime of serving the public's whims and fancies.

Lloyd stopped drumming his fingers long enough to pick up a pen and start tapping the capped end on a weekly organizer pad. *Stupid Stuff I Gotta*

Do This Week. He tapped number three. Call the Steadman. "Yes, I was calling on the off chance you might have a room available for the next two or three days. I know this is rather short notice, but this was a spur of the moment idea." The lie tasted funny.

"If you'll allow me just one moment, I'll be happy to check for you, sir. I believe we may have a room available tonight. Could you hold please?"

"Yes."

The line went silent. At that moment the idea of severing the connection before the reservations clerk returned was overwhelming. Though he needed to go back, this might not be the time. Maybe in a couple of months. That's it, he thought. I'll wait a little longer.

With that thought in mind he reached for the plunger. Just as the voice returned. "Sir, we have an ocean view room available, and I will be more than happy to hold it for you if you'd like."

Lloyd hesitated. He was still not one hundred percent sure about this decision.

"Sir…"

"Oh… right. That will be fine." He fished for his American Express card. "I'm sorry if I sound a little out of it. To tell you the truth, I wasn't sure you would even be open. I thought I remembered someone telling me you were in the process of remodeling."

"No sir, that's all finished. We are right here and ready for your visit."

"OK, that sounds fine. My name is Lloyd McPherson, and my American Express number is—"

"Mr. McPherson, you of all people don't need to secure a room. You're a valued guest here, and it will be our pleasure to have you stay with us again. As a matter of fact, I look forward to serving you personally."

Lloyd sat back in his chair. "Thank you, that's very kind. I'm looking forward to staying…

another lie?

…for a few days. I will probably arrive sometime after nine tonight."

The voice, smooth as polished wood. "We'll be waiting. Have a pleasant trip."

The world went dark again. "Thank you."

"Good bye then, Mr. McPherson."

"Goodbye."

Lloyd replaced the receiver and stared at the telephone. Stared like a man waiting for the next word from God Himself.

•

The open road and the subliminal hint of salt in the air cleared his head a little. Lloyd had been driving for almost an hour and a half before he so much as sighed. He hadn't sung with the radio, hadn't even yelled at the Volkswagen full of college kids that pulled out in front of him earlier. His silent grief had been gray and deep, just like the weather. But even with the thickening clouds overhead, the sea air began to work its magic. Slowly. So slowly.

He and Carrington had always loved the beach. Before they could afford a place on the ocean, they dreamed of having their own place. Then, when money was no problem, they found they enjoyed going to various hotels or renting a condo for a week or two. That way they could enjoy one another and somebody else could worry about maintenance, grass cutting, and all the other little headaches that go with owning their own place.

And now the ocean was starting to soothe him somewhat. But not before he had replayed the events of their last day together.

They had read about the Steadman Resort in a regional travel magazine and immediately fell in love with it. The tennis courts, racquetball courts, ocean view, bicycle trails, and attentive staff were just the tip of the iceberg. The location—the Outer Banks of North Carolina—was secluded enough to afford them privacy when they wanted it, but they were close enough to the quaint shops and historic sights of the surrounding area to immerse themselves to the fullest. And immerse themselves they had.

Their days had been filled with walks on secluded beaches, picnics on the shore, treks to such exotic places as Duck and Nags Head, and wonderful evenings of dinner, dancing, and romance. The resort had a grand ballroom and an orchestra that played big band and swing music until the wee hours of the morning. They had enjoyed their first trip so much they had spent the past five Thanksgivings there.

Almost five.

Every newspaper in the state ran a story about the fire. Due to the tragic outcome, it even made the wire services. Fifty people lost their lives and a dozen more went to the hospital with various cuts, burns, and broken bones. The news people said it was lucky anybody survived at all.

But Lloyd McPherson hadn't felt lucky.

The fire started on the outside of the building and effectively trapped everyone in the ballroom from the start. At first no one noticed. It was Thanksgiving and the Steadman was hosting its annual black tie charity dinner and dance. Champagne. Party favors. The works. The orchestra had been playing an arrangement of *Woodchopper's Ball* that had two thirds of the couples in attendance on the dance floor. The large hearth at one end of the room—so big you could roast an entire pig in it—crackled and snapped while the celebrants whirled and glided across the room.

Blanche Lee was the first to notice that something was wrong. She noticed the moment the window next to her shattered from the heat outside. An eighteen-inch dagger of glass pinned her to her chair and claimed the first casualty.

Marge Newland, Blanche's newfound friend and fellow antique shop aficionado, screamed as the shards of glass fell around her. She watched her companion die in horrible slow motion. Time was molasses thick and through it all Marge could neither move nor breathe. The scream siphoned all the air from her lungs and the effort to refill them was thwarted by panic. She started to hyperventilate.

At the same time Marge screamed, Joe Ramey burned his hand on the door which led to the outer hallway and on to the main building. The massive oak door blistered his hand, but his yelp of pain had been lost in the scream of Marge Newland. Later that night Joe would tell district fire chief Walt Richards about the ensuing pandemonium after himself rescuing five people from the blazing ruin.

All Lloyd remembered from that point on was trying to get himself and Carrington out of the building. When the severity of the situation hit home, the herd instinct took over and the occupants of the room all headed for an exit. Joe waved them away from the door which had devoured two layers of skin moments earlier, and the crowd shifted toward the next exit. Caught in the crush, he and Carrington had been swept along with the tide. Stumbling, sweat soaked hands slipping but never completely losing contact. They scanned the room for another way out.

When the line that fed the gas jets in the fireplace ruptured, the orchestra was as good as dead. The resulting explosion unfolded a fan of solid blue flame that covered the entire bandstand. So intense was the blaze that the lead trumpet player's valve oil bottle erupted in his hand and created a blue hot formal length glove of flame. Elbow to fingertips. Nobody heard him scream.

Overhead a beam exploded and several others ignited as if by an unseen hand. The crowd, very much like stampeding cattle, finally found an exit and began to trample one another in an effort to leave the microcosm of hell. Pushing and shoving. Trampling anything and anyone in their path.

It was at that point the beam above Lloyd started to fall.

His first instinct had been to pull Carrington to safety, and he had pulled with all his might.

He had pulled against the tide of terrified humanity.

He had pulled against the tide of the inevitable.

In the seconds that seemed to stretch into months, he saw her face. Saw the look of horror on that smudged, perfect face. Somehow her cheek had been cut and the blood seemed to have been painted on in a long thin line from ear to chin. Then time suddenly sped up, a demon train on its way to oblivion. He remembered screaming her name, remembered being shoved deeper into the crowd, remembered the feeling as their fingers slipped apart. And he remembered the beam falling. Flame brushed oak, and close to a thousand pounds of flame and timber, came crashing down with an ear-splitting roar. He remembered thinking at the time it sounded like a victory cry. In the end, it had killed four people. Carrington and three others.

He could remember screaming and trying to wade against the frightened, cow-eyed mass of people, but he couldn't remember how he managed to get out. And at this moment, watching the world through a haze of tears, he didn't know how long he had been in the Steadman parking area.

Lloyd switched off the Jaguar's engine, unbuckled his seat belt, and got out of the car. The last half hour was a blur. He still thought about that night often enough, but it had been a while since the memory had been that vivid. Was that an omen? A message to retreat for a while longer? He didn't know. Couldn't bring himself to think about it now.

The first thing he noticed when he entered the lobby was the sameness of it. It hadn't changed one bit. The wood, the furnishings, the plants, even the smell. Brass polish and heart pine. It was as if the Steadman had never burned.

The sound of the bellman's voice jolted him back to reality. "May I be of service, sir?" A voice accustomed to helping travelers caught up in the spell of the Steadman. No impatience. Just waiting to do his job; a job he had no doubt performed since the Steadman's opening.

"No. I mean yes. I need to check in. My reservation is in the name McPherson."

The bellman took the lone suitcase. "Of course, Mr. McPherson. We've been expecting you." He bowed ever so slightly. "Please follow me."

Lloyd was escorted to the front desk where he was greeted like an old friend. "Mr. McPherson," the desk clerk said. "I trust you had an enjoyable drive." He nodded to the bellman. "Take Mr. McPherson's case to his room."

He turned to tell his escort he would be glad to handle his own bag, but the bellman and his suitcase had disappeared.

"Mr. McPherson, here is the key. You will be in room one thirty-nine. If there is anything else you need, please don't hesitate to ring the desk." Lloyd turned and accepted the brass key. He looked at it, trying to find the answer to a question as yet unformed.

"Mr. McPherson, is there a problem?"

"No. No, I was just—" He looked at the desk manager. "Just trying to get over how perfect everything is. It's almost as if the Steadman never, well, never—"

The desk manager smiled. "I know. It is quite astounding what can be done when you want it badly enough."

"True enough I suppose. It's funny though." Lloyd looked at the key again. Noticed how the light rippled across the polished brass. "I didn't realize you had rebuilt the entire complex."

The desk manager, his voice as smooth as the polished wood of the hotel, smiled. "Well, you have been rather preoccupied, if I may be so bold." The smile changed ever so slightly.

"No," Lloyd answered, "you're absolutely right." He pocketed the key and stepped back from the desk. "I think a few days here might actually be just the thing I need to—"

The desk manager cut him off. "Of course. We understand completely. This cannot be an easy journey for you." The smile slipped away. "So sad. So tragic and so sad."

Lloyd nodded but said nothing. Another sound had captured his attention. A sound he really hadn't expected. It was music. Big band music. He looked around to his left then back again. "You really have made a comeback." He looked in the direction from which strains of "I Can't Get Started" flowed.

"Maybe you'd care to have a drink and listen to the orchestra for a while before you turn in Mr. McPherson. I believe you will find it beneficial."

Lloyd started to refuse the suggestion and go straight to his room. The trip had been long and he wasn't sure he was ready to go in the ballroom just yet. He was just now becoming accustomed to the idea that he was here and having a conversation with the desk manager. In fact, he realized he had not had his credit card imprinted or even inquired about the man's name.

He turned to raise the issues with the desk manager but was stopped short. The blond man behind the counter extended his hand, and Lloyd shook it automatically. "Now Mr. McPherson, you go right in, order a drink, and make yourself comfortable. Don't be concerned about your room. We will take perfect care of you. And should you need anything, ask for me personally. My name is Paul."

The room seemed to tilt slightly, and he followed the tilt toward the room where the orchestra played. He turned back just long enough for Paul to say, "Go in sir. This is the reason you came."

Before he could respond, his hand was on the brass door handle and he was inside.

The room was exactly the way he remembered it. The long mahogany bar to his right was polished to a high sheen. The brass rails and sparkling glass and crystal ware reflected in the long mirror behind the bar created the illusion of a huge double bar. And the single bar was plenty large for the room.

The tables were arranged in clusters around a pristine dance floor, recently polished to a high gloss. There were already about fifty couples in various sections of the room. The orchestra played as if there was a New Year's party in full swing. The bandleader threw a two-fingered salute in Lloyd's direction while giving the downbeat for "Satin Doll."

"How many in your party, sir?"

Lloyd turned to the woman who addressed him. Her platinum hair and fair skin was a perfect contrast to her night-black dress. "Just one, thank you."

"Will anyone be joining you later?"

Lloyd cocked his head as if he hadn't understood. "No, I'm alone this evening." *That's the truth if I ever told it,* he thought as he was escorted to a table near the bandstand. When he was seated, the platinum vision in black took his drink order and went back to the bar.

For the first time since his arrival, Lloyd had a chance to really look and take everything in. It was the same. From the exposed beams right down to the design in the carpet. It was exactly the same. Like the desk manager had said, it was amazing what you could do if you wanted to badly enough.

If only that were really true.

A slight movement at his right elbow interrupted his thoughts. "That didn't take very long," he said as he turned to take his drink.

"No, not long at all," Carrington said in response.

Carrington.

The room shifted, slightly out of focus. Lloyd could see nothing except the face of his beloved Carrington.

Carrington was dead.

Impossible. She died here.

Heart hammering. Hard to breathe. Room spinning.

Lloyd's heart jackhammered his ribs. Cold.

Oh dear God, he thought. I'm losing it.

He closed his eyes and tried to bring his breathing under control. Calm. Deeper, deeper. There now. He opened his eyes. The specter of his dead wife was gone. Stress, he thought. That's what it is. I just came out too soon.

He turned to pick up his glass. If he ever needed a drink, he needed one now.

"Lloyd."

The sound of his name turned his spine to ice.

Carrington sat across from him looking for all the world the way she had looked the day they first came to the Steadman.

He looked at her. Saw without fully comprehending. The face was the same. The same delicate nose; the same bright green eyes. The same porcelain skin. It was Carrington.

But it couldn't be.

"What's happening to me?" Lloyd asked no one in particular. A last attempt to hold his emotions in a safety net. "What's happening?"

Carrington smiled. "Don't you know? Really?"

Lloyd slid his chair back and jerked his hands away from the table as if it had carried a two-twenty charge. "This is not happening. It's not." A tear formed in the corner of one eye. "It's not."

The smile changed ever so slightly. "Yes it is, Lloyd. This is happening. Everything here is perfect. Just the way you wanted it."

The words were lost on him.

"How? I mean…I…" He looked around the room. The orchestra played—had never stopped playing—while couples danced, or sat and listened. Ice tinkled in glasses. Smoke from a dozen cigarettes ambled toward the ceiling.

Smoke.

Fire.

Then.

Now.

"No. This is wrong. All wrong."

"Why," she asked. "It's what you wanted."

"What I wanted?" He turned to face what had once been his partner in life. "What do you mean this is what I wanted?"

"Lloyd, I know you've been hurting. Every day since—"

"No." He cut her off and shook his head. "I came here to come to terms with what happened." He sent a less than steady hand to fetch his drink.

"Is that really why you came?"

The bourbon was tasteless. There was no reassuring jolt of initial fire from throat to belly. He looked at the glass, then at his wife. "What?"

"You came here hoping to find it had all been a dream. You wanted the impossible to happen, and now it has." She held out a hand. "Now you have to accept it."

He moved his chair toward the table. Hesitated. His heart was a thoroughbred straining against the gate.

"Carrington?"

The tear traced its way down his cheek. Many more followed the path it blazed.

"Carrington…how…I mean…how did…?"

"You did it."

The words hit him with the force of a sledge hammer. "How did I do this? How could I possibly?"

"If you want something bad enough." She smiled again. The smile he had seen a thousand times. The smile that brought the reality of the situation home.

He reached for her hand. "It really is you. You're here." Now it was his turn to smile. "It's impossible, but you're here."

She nodded. "I told you so."

He looked at her. Really looked at her. He couldn't help himself. She was exactly as she had always been. Perfect.

He released her hand and wiped the tears from his eyes. The orchestra played and couples swirled around the floor. But as far as he was concerned, there was no one else in the world but Carrington. His Carrington. It was absolutely impossible and absolutely true. He stood and walked around the table.

"Can I hold you?"

The orchestra played a slow Glenn Miller tune. Carrington stood.

"Yes."

Lloyd took her in his arms. Savored the feel of her. He buried his face in the soft junction of her neck and shoulder. Pulled her closer. All the memories and all the suppressed feelings rushed back in a solid wall of emotion. She was here. They were together. And she felt

If you want something bad enough

different.

He held her tighter.

She didn't respond.

He held her at arm's length. "Carrington, what's wrong?"

She smiled again. The same smile he had loved for years. The same? Almost the same.

"Just then when I held you. Didn't you feel anything at all?"

"No. We don't feel anything here."

He bit his lower lip. Partly habit and partly for the pain. He needed to clear his head. "What do you mean you don't feel anything here?"

She motioned for him to sit. "When I passed over I saw the fire, the smoke, the crush of people. And I saw others around me watching the same thing. Then there was nothing for a while. I knew what was happening, but it didn't matter."

Lloyd's head was spinning. The orchestra continued to play and the couples continued to swirl. Then he realized what had bothered him from the moment he walked in. With the exception of the desk manager and the hostess, no one had spoken. The couples at the tables smoked and drank but never uttered a word. The orchestra played but there was no banter between songs from the bandleader.

"You see, we know everything we need to know here. This is a different level of existence, so the physical amenities of the other existence really aren't necessary."

"If you don't have any feelings for me then why did you come back?" The tears started again but this time there was no trickle.

"Lloyd, I didn't come back. You came to me. What you see is the essence of who I was. Much like it was frozen in time. We do not age, we do not feel. We know what we need to know. We exist, and existence is enough."

He attempted to understand. "Then this is Heaven?"

"No."

"Is it Hell?"

"No."

Lloyd felt the first stirring of anger push his fear off to the side. "Then where are we?"

"We're at the Steadman. Your Steadman."

The black dawning of complete realization struck him full and hard.

"Carrington, you said there were others watching the events of that night with you. Do you mean these—"

She nodded.

He began to shiver. The air had grown suddenly cold and the fire in the hearth provided no warmth. He watched the couples swirl soundlessly. The orchestra played on, no longer burned by the inferno, no longer feeling the music. Just shades of musicians playing shades of feelings long forgotten.

"If what you say is true then I'm going back home. If I can't hold you—the real you—then I won't settle for the substitute. I just can't."

She took his arm. "You can't leave."

Another smile. Mirthless. The memory of a smile. "Those who haven't crossed over know so little. You assume it is always those from this side who cross over. Hauntings, you call them." She paused.

If you want something bad enough, you can make it happen

"Sometimes one of you crosses over to here. That's what you did." She sounded so matter-of-fact now.

"There is no front desk. No Steadman. And tomorrow or the day after, someone will find your car parked where you left it. In front of the charred foundation of what used to be the Steadman Resort."

Lloyd's breath caught in his throat. The room grew colder. The band played louder. He grabbed her shoulders and shouted to be heard above the orchestra. "You mean I'll just stay here, never age, and keep company with a room full of what used to be?"

"Not exactly. You'll age, but since time has so little meaning here, you will age slowly. But you will never die." She smiled her dead smile.

The horror of the situation bloomed, a blood rose opening in his mind. He would age beyond ancient with the specter of his fondest memory eternally before him. Never changing. Never caring. The realization was too much. He pushed what had been the love of his life aside and raced toward the nearest exit.

He turned the brass door handle and rushed toward the lobby and his waiting car.

The room was exactly the way he remembered it. The long mahogany bar to his right was polished to a high sheen. The brass rails and sparkling glass and crystal ware reflected in the long mirror behind the bar created the illusion of a huge double bar. And the single bar was plenty large for the room.

The tables were arranged in clusters around a pristine dance floor, recently polished to a high gloss. There were already about fifty couples in various sections of the room. The orchestra played as if there was a New Year's party in full swing. The bandleader threw a two-fingered salute in Lloyd's direction while giving the downbeat for "Satin Doll."

"How many in your party, sir?"

Lloyd turned to the woman who addressed him. Her platinum hair and fair skin were a perfect contrast to her night-black dress.

He couldn't speak. Undiluted dread clutched his throat with fingers of cold glass bone.

"Will anyone be joining you later?"

He heard a soft click as the door closed behind him.

"Yes."

Former Wear

"I really hate to do this," Elmo said as he stuffed his jaw full of Beechnut chewing tobacco. He hitched his pants up a notch and leaned on the shovel in his right hand. "Somehow it just don't seem right."

Tillmer Faye Earwood, matriarch of the Earwood clan, held up a hand that hadn't seen soap or water for more than a few days. "Look Elmo, I didn't plan on having to do this anymore than you did." She ran a hand through her stringy gray hair. "But after all, this is for Percy. And Lord knows he don't hardly ever ask for much." She pointed toward the seventeen-year-old boy standing off to the side. He was a dead ringer for Ichabod Crane; a skinny series of odd angles, elbows, bony knees, size thirteen feet, and ears that looked like two saucers glued to the side of his head. Percy looked at his cousin from under his mop of red hair and grinned.

"I know," Elmo said, "but—"

"But nothing Elmo," Tillmer Faye said as she took a step toward him. "The discussion is over and the situation is what it is. Now are you gonna dance with that shovel, or dig with it."

Elmo swung the shovel over his shoulder. "Well, I'll tell you," he said around the toothpick in his mouth. "If I was to dance with it, I'd have a sight more to hang on to than Selma will when she grabs hold of old dry bones over there." He motioned with his head and grinned.

Tillmer Faye shot him a look that could have boiled water.

Elmo dug.

Within an hour and a half, the grave was open and the casket was laid parallel to the six-by-six hole. Percy stood in one spot the whole time, a brown parcel clamped to his chest. Tillmer Faye had told him to be careful not to let anything happen to the store-bought package, and it was always best to do what Tillmer Faye said.

"Lord God a'mighty," Elmo said as he wiped his face with an old bandana. "Grandpa Earwood has gotten a might ripe over the last three weeks." He blew his nose and put the bandana back in his pocket. "And he wasn't exactly the first rose of spring on his best day."

"Elmo," Tillmer Faye said, "you know Grandpa Earwood has always had a little problem with how he smelled. But he's family, and when you're family, you just kinda overlook these things."

Percy stepped a little closer as Elmo levered the casket lid open. Grandpa's pent-up essence escaped the confines of his eternal resting place in full force. Percy sputtered. "Mama, grandpa was rank enough when he was alive, what with him being partial to just takin' a bath on Saturday and all. But now he plumb stinks." He stepped back a step and coughed. "I mean golly Moses; I don't want to go to my first prom smellin' like I stepped in something." He hung his head.

"I wish old Selma Mudge hadn't asked me now."

Tillmer bent over the casket and started to work. "Well, she did, and you're going." She looked up. "You're the first Earwood to ever go to a fancy dance. So, Elmo," she looked toward the big man leaning on his shovel, "help me get this tuxedo off grandpa. And Percy, unwrap them pajamas. Then we'll go home and hang this monkey suit out on the porch to air out until it's time for you to get dressed."

Mother and Child Reunion

Eddie Grant watched the clock on the kitchen wall while his mother lit another Marlboro. She had only been in the house five minutes and was already chain smoking. Some things never changed. She had always managed to find something to hide behind—vague excuses, a cloud of smoke, whatever was handy. Couple that with the fact that he had been away for a while, and they never really communicated very much in the past anyway, and the sum of the equation was less than encouraging.

Becky Grant blew a column of smoke toward the ceiling at the same time her son Eddie cleared his throat. She looked at him—really looked at him—for the first time in a long time. She saw the hard profile of a young man, formed from the face of the young boy she remembered.

He felt her stare; felt her taking him in.

Shoulder length dishwater blond hair, sharp nose, and thin, hard-set lips. More than once he had heard her say how lucky he was that he resembled her side of the family and not his father's, the son of a bitch.

Every time she talked about his father, she followed it up with "son of a bitch," and as far as he was concerned, she was right. But that was all behind him now. All over.

Her voice brought him back to the here and now. "Eddie? Eddie, are you OK?" She was leaning across the battered Formica table, the smell of cigarette smoke heavy on her breath. She touched his arm and he pulled away.

"Yeah, I'm OK," he said. He turned his head slightly to the right so he could see her a little better.

"I was real surprised to hear from you after all these years. I don't even know how you found me."

"What's the matter?" he asked. "Didn't you want to be found?" His voice was ice.

Becky Grant sat back in her chair. Stubbed her cigarette in the ashtray balanced on her left knee, the ghost of a Holiday Inn logo still visible under the residue of age and nicotine. "What do you mean by that? Of course I'm glad you found me."

Eddie settled back to his original position. "That's not what I asked."

Night was starting to settle just outside the dingy window. The advancing gloomlight spread shadows over the landscape of dirty dishes in the sink. Evening was on its way and time was of the essence. There would be no second chance to make everything right.

Neither spoke for a long moment. Mother and son sat in dark silence, contemplating their next move in this familial chess match.

Eddie broke the silence.

"You just disappeared. Gone without so much as a kissmyass, go blind, or anything." His throat tightened with the effort of actually saying the words. His eyes narrowed a fraction. He turned back to face her, his face a mass of shadows. "You just left me, goddammit. Eight years old, and you just left." He turned back to face the clock on the wall, his mood and profile darkening by degrees.

Becky leaned forward and reached for Eddie's arm and the ashtray clattered to the floor. Neither seemed to notice.

She spoke, and he pulled away from her again. The fabric of his leather jacket was cold, and the cold seemed to creep into her tone of voice. "Left you? Is that what you thought? That I left you? I didn't…"

He cut in. "Left, abandoned, call it whatever you want to." He was little more than an extension of the shadows around him now.

Once again Becky extended her hand toward him. This time, however, instead of touching him, she jabbed the Formica tabletop with her index finger for emphasis. "Well let me tell you a little something. You're not the only one involved here. You're not the only one in this family who has had it rough, and if you'll listen for a minute, I'll tell you why I did what I did."

Eddie shrugged. "I don't expect an explanation. I just think it's time to make things right."

"Well then listen to me and maybe we can." She lit another cigarette, picked up the fallen ashtray, settled back in her chair, and launched a column of smoke into the room. "I never planned to marry your father, the son of a bitch. The hard cold fact is one night we went to a party and had too much to drink. One thing led to another, and I wound up pregnant. That was you."

She paused to take another drag and watch her son for a reaction. There was none.

Becky continued. "We argued for two days. Finally, your father said he would marry me. The son of a bitch thought he was doing me a big favor. But feeding his big-assed ego is what he was doing. He didn't want any of his buddies to think he couldn't take care of his mistakes. They were his exact words: *'Take care of my mistakes.'* "We were married later that month. Ran off to South Carolina and had a honeymoon, if you can call it that, at South of the Border. We ate bad Mexican food, bought fireworks, and came home the next day."

Eddie remembered home. A dirty little trailer in a dirty little trailer park. More than anything else he remembered the walls of his home; walls so thin you could hear everything that went on in the surrounding rooms.

Everything.

Becky got up and walked over to the windowsill to retrieve a book of matches she had seen earlier. She felt around for a light switch.

"Can we turn on a light? It's getting dark."

Eddie didn't move. "I like it this way. Besides, this won't take long."

She headed back to the KMart special chair on her side of the table. "OK," she said as she lit the next cigarette. "Where were we?"

Eddie looked at the clock. "Home."

"Oh yeah," she said. "Home. It sure didn't seem like much of one, did it?" He didn't rise to her attempt at bonding. She paused a second and continued.

"I had always pictured something much different. I always thought there would be romance, love, and a little house with a picket fence and a garden. You know?" Now she was speaking to no one in particular. Her voice had taken on a softer quality. But that, like the waning light, was short-lived.

"Yeah, that's what I wanted. But what I got was shitty diapers, a shitty house, and a shitty life."

Eddie turned to fully face his mother for the first time in nine years. "Yeah, well we all got more than we bargained for, and personally I'm not real impressed with your story so far. Big damn deal. You had to put up with a little shit. Well, whoopty doo. What we're dealing with here is family and the truth, not some fairy tale world. Truth."

The venom in her son's words hit the target, and he knew it. This was what he came for. Truth.

Becky Grant did not disappoint her son. She half stood, palms supporting her weight on the table. "OK, you want it this way, we'll do it this way. Yeah. I put up with shit, but I put up with more than a little. I put up with a ton of it. I put up with your father's drunken rages, his alternate beatings and tit squeezings, his cheap shots at what he called the piece he married, and his taking off for days at a time and leaving me with no car, no money, and two crying kids."

She paused to let the anger dissipate or increase, whichever it chose. In the meantime, three matches broke before she was able to light the next cigarette. Becky was running on pure disappointment and high-test hate.

"You said you wanted truth. OK, truth it is." She sighed, and out it came. "I hated you and your sister. I realize now that it wasn't your fault, but back then I just wanted you both gone. And since that wasn't possible, I figured my being gone was the next best thing."

"What did we ever do to you?"

Becky spread her hands. "You didn't do anything. It's just that every time I looked at you both, all I saw was him. All I felt was him forcing himself on me. I smelled his sour breath and felt his rough hands. You were part of him, and that was enough."

Eddie settled back into his seat. Content in the fact that she was hiding behind all kinds of smoke now.

It was almost time.

Becky was back in her seat, but she still leaned forward as if waiting for another shot from the boy across from her.

None came.

"Eddie, why are we doing this? I haven't seen you or your sister for nine years..."

"She has a name."

Becky stopped short. "I know your sister's name, but Connie isn't the issue here. You are."

Eddie glanced at the clock and turned to his mother. "Mother dear, I'm afraid you're wrong about that."

Almost time.

"We were part of him, but we were part of you too, and you left us. That was the worst part. You didn't even stop to consider that we were part of you too."

"Baby, that's not true." Her voice lost some of its edge. "At first I was glad to be away from all of it. You, Connie, him, everything. Then later I tried to get you back, but by then you had all moved. And I didn't have the money to find you."

"You still could have taken us with you." The seventeen-year-old voice carried all the hurt and disappointment its years could hold.

Her shoulders dropped with the increase, rather than the removal of, an invisible weight. Her head rocked back and forth.

It was almost time.

"Eddie, you don't understand." Tears brimming. "You don't—"

The words exploded. "Like Hell I don't. Do you remember who you left us with? Huh? Did you think he was just going to suddenly realize the error of his ways and mellow out when he found out you were gone? Huh? Did you think the abuse would stop? Did you?" He was on his feet now. Eyes aglow, fury rising. "Let me tell you *my* story, mom." The venom was back, stronger than he expected. “Let me tell you about beatings. Let me tell you about being left alone for days on end.” He leaned on the table and looked directly into his mother’s face.

“Let me tell you about a father’s drunken midnight visits to his little daughter’s room. You want to hear the details? Huh? I had to hear them. He might have locked me in my room, but he couldn’t lock everything out. You want to hear about *that*?”

Understanding waited just beyond the shadows. “Oh my God. Baby, I didn’t know. I didn’t…” Understanding dawned. Her expression changed. “Midnight visits? You don’t mean he…” The shadow that was her son nodded.

“Connie, oh dear God, where is Connie.”

Eddie shook his head. “She’s nearby. And for the first time in a long time, she’s OK. Or at least as OK as she can be.” He sat down and motioned for his mother to do the same.

Seven ten.

Almost time.

Five more minutes.

He heard sirens in the distance and started to smile. This wasn’t the safest neighborhood in town, but it was better than the trailer.

The color drained out of Becky’s face. The cigarette she held between her fingers dropped to the floor unnoticed. “Near? How near?”

“Upstairs.”

Becky stood and headed toward the living room. She turned in every direction, looking for the door that would lead her to the stairs, and ultimately to her estranged daughter.

“Connie. Connie, baby. It’s me. It’s mamma. Come on down honey and let me see you.”

In the midst of her urgent dance, she sensed the hand on her arm more than felt it. “Don’t. She won’t answer.”

The whirling mother stopped. “What do you mean she won’t answer? I’m her mother for Pete’s sake. Of course she’ll answer.” She attempted to pull away. “Connie, come on down and let’s talk.”

Becky found herself being brought back into the kitchen. Though part of her wanted to find her daughter, part of her couldn't resist the pull of her son.

"Sit down."

Becky looked around, bewildered, and followed his directions. Between the sirens outside, the realization that her daughter was in the house, and her son's strange behavior, things were starting to move too fast for her. "I want to see Connie. I want..."

"It's a little late for what you want. In fact, it's almost too late."

"Too late? What do you mean too late?"

Eddie reached in his jacket pocket and placed a white bundle on the table. "I mean that Connie called the police the minute she saw you drive up. Then I shot her."

"You what?" Her breath caught in her throat like bad meat.

Eddie fingered the hole just behind his right ear. His hair covered the entrance wound fairly well, but the exit wound was a bit harder to conceal. The evening shadows and his mother's state of mind had helped.

"I shot her. Like I told you, I came to make things right." The sirens were a little louder now. "You see, this is where we moved after you left, when you couldn't find us. It isn't much, but it sure beats that trailer." His laugh was hard and cold. "It's much quieter. But enough chit chat. I don't have much time."

Becky looked at her son as if he was a bug under a magnifying glass.

"Like I said, I found out today Connie is pregnant."

A small sob formed in Becky Grant's throat. "You mean?"

"Yes. Daddy." The horror of the situation was starting to come home. "Now be quiet. This takes a lot of effort." Eddie was starting to fade into the shadows. "Open the handkerchief."

Unable to do much more than follow directions, Connie's mother exposed the Taurus nine-millimeter pistol. "What?"

"Like I told you. It's to make everything right. When daddy came home from the plant, I confronted him. Told the bastard that I knew what he had done, and then shot him. Next, Connie and I spent the rest of the morning working out the rest of the details."

Becky picked up the pistol, and turned it over in her hands, fascinated. Unable to speak.

He continued. "So, mother dear, it's probably just as well she can't answer you. I don't think you would have liked what she had to say."

The sirens were louder now.

"When you drove up, Connie dialed 911 and reported a shooting. Since this is the wrong side of the tracks, it takes about twelve to fifteen minutes minimum for the police to come to this part of town. After she hung up, I put a pillow over her head and shot her. She was smiling for the first time in years." He paused to give the statement full impact.

"Then I shot myself. I timed it with your closing the car door.

"In about a minute the police are going to come in here and find three bodies upstairs, and a gun with your fingerprints all over it downstairs."

Becky, teetering on the edge of sanity, dropped the pistol. "Why, Eddie? Why?"

"Because, mother. You were the only one who could have stopped it. You could have taken us with you."

She shook her head. "No, son. I couldn't have done anything. I didn't know."

There was a knock at the door.

"Daddy made life a living hell. And we were just kids. We couldn't do anything but endure every day, hoping beyond hope that it would be the last. But you; you had an out. You could have done something."

Knocking again.

Louder.

Voices.

"Open up. Police."

"I believe that's for you." Eddie was fading.

Becky Grant stood up, took a step toward the next room, and turned back toward the kitchen.

Her outstretched hand reached toward empty shadows.

A Grail By Any Other Name

Head down, hands stuffed in his overcoat pockets, hair fighting a losing battle with the wind, Dr. Joseph Lineberger walked toward Emory University.

He had been enthusiastic about the weekend conference at first, at least as enthusiastic as he ever allowed himself to be. Three days of lectures, presentations, and major archaeological finds on display, some for the first time. This had been his world. His life.

In another time and place, far removed from his present life, he would have relished the chance to be an integral part of such an event.

In another time.

The extent of his excitement today, however, was the fact that he had actually eaten lunch in a very pleasant restaurant instead of having to eat at home to the accompaniment of his wife's endless stream of woes.

There's never enough money. You never take me anywhere. You mouse, show some backbone. People take advantage of you left and right. Why don't you move ahead like your colleagues? THEY show some initiative. Do you enjoy embarrassing me, or do you just not care about tenure? On and on she harped. Played the same tune night and day.

After a while, he just stopped listening. He had the answers down pat, so he just nodded and muttered the usual, "You're right dear. I'll try harder."

Inevitably, thoughts of his life surrounded him as surely as the gathering clouds surround the elements of a storm.

Had the weather been clear and fair, it wouldn't have made any difference. For the last ten years, time and circumstances had taken their toll on his mind, body, and spirit. Joseph Lineberger, unimportant professor of archaeology at an unimportant college, in an unimportant town in West Virginia, always walked as if the burden he carried inside was actually on his shoulders. He wore his disillusionment—the quintessence of his life—like a funeral shroud, and on this particular day he had his unseen cloak pulled tightly around himself.

He had been so involved in the clash between temporary freedom and the dreary certainty of the life which awaited him back home that the first heavy raindrops, harbingers of the coming storm, went completely unnoticed. So preoccupied was he that he didn't realize he was getting soaked until a peal of thunder jarred him back to reality. The rain was falling in thick, black sheets, and the wind had picked up so much that the rain seemed to be falling sideways.

The slight professor, glasses spotted and streaked by this point, hunched his shoulders against the cold rain and felt inside the huge overcoat pockets for his hat. He realized while his hands continued their search that he had decided to forego the rolled-up hat since Minerva wasn't there to conduct her final inspection.

"My God," she would say, *"do you need somebody to watch you every single minute? Where's your hat?"* Then she would get the exasperated look on her face, the one that made him want to strangle her. *"Don't you know what those black things in the sky mean? My God, you are hopeless."*

Now he wished he had been a little less defiant. Damn, he hated it when she was even a little bit right about these things. Sometimes it made him think, if only for a moment, that she just might be right.

As if in cahoots with his wife, reality played a cruel trick. Dr. Joseph Lineberger realized that he didn't know where he was. He recognized neither the street nor any of the buildings that rose up around him, half shadowed by storm and gloom. Nothing looked familiar. The rational side of his mind tried to convince him that it was just the suddenness of the storm and the canopy of black clouds that had him momentarily confused, but instinctively he knew that he was lost.

Since the rain wasn't about to let up, the most logical thing to do was to find shelter. The archaeologist trotted toward a canopied doorway sandwiched between a shop which advertised rare books and another storefront which showed all the signs of being abandoned. Once under the awning, he took a moment to brush the rain off of his coat sleeves, producing a miniature shower of his own. Next, he ran his fingers through his thinning hair creating still another shower.

Joseph Lineberger turned to peer into the triangular glass pane embedded in the top portion of the wooden door. Though there was a light on, the interior was blurred. At first, he thought he was looking through faceted glass, but the illusion was created by the wet lenses of his glasses.

While he tried to find a dry surface on which to clear his lenses, the professor mentally retraced his steps as best he could. How could he possibly have gotten lost no farther than he was from the campus? There was no logical explanation as far as he could determine. Wouldn't Minerva have a great time at his expense if she ever found out.

"My God," she would say in a whine that consisted of one-part fingernails on a chalkboard and two parts AM radio static. *"How can a grown man, even a grown man like you, get lost three blocks from the school?"*

Right again Minerva, he thought as he wiped his glasses on the handkerchief he had found in his inner coat pocket. He wasn't certain whether it was the sudden tinkling of bells or the old man's voice that caused him to drop his glasses.

Joseph Lineberger drew a sharp breath, dropped his glasses, and jerked his head up all at the same time. The figure, which stood before him in the now open doorway, was a bit hazy, but he could make out what appeared to be a small man, old, with a striking shock of white hair.

"My goodness professor, I didn't mean to startle you," said the man as he bent over to retrieve the fallen spectacles. The worn welcome mat on which they landed prevented any major damage. The older gentleman handed the glasses to their startled owner and continued. "Here," he said with a trace of a German accent. "I hope they are not damaged."

"Why no," Dr. Lineberger said as he gave them one more wipe for good measure. "They appear to be just fine. I'm the one who's a bit shaken up."

"Again, I apologize. Please, come in and avail yourself of my humble facilities. They are not fancy, but they are warm and you are soaked to the bone." The white-haired gentleman grasped the slightly younger man's arm and ushered him inside. Though still somewhat perplexed, warm and dry prevailed over wet and cold and Joseph Lineberger stepped into the old man's shop.

As the door closed behind them, Joseph heard the tinkling of the bell over the door again. The shop was not as well lighted as he first thought, and the air inside seemed heavier; dense to the point of being almost tangible. There was a musty smell so pervasive he could almost taste it. It was the smell of decay, but there was a bitter sweetness just below the surface. Repulsive, and at the same time, inviting. His head was still reeling from the initial scare, and the sudden change of atmosphere only made matters worse.

The strange little man guided him to a high-backed chair upholstered in a deep, dark, red velvet. Once Joseph was seated comfortably—as comfortably as he could be—his unexpected benefactor sat across from him in an identical chair.

As his eyes adjusted to the gloom, the professor realized that he must be in an antique shop of some sort. Just to his right was a small writing desk complete with a silver inkstand with a crow quill. Off to his left, some distance away, stood a suit of armor complete with sword and lance. There were books with exquisite leather bindings inlaid with gold. There were figurines, desks, chairs, paintings, and jewelry. Clothes, paperweights, maps, and documents of all sorts.

The old man smiled while the professor continued his stationary tour of the little shop. Globes, trunks, and pewter ware, all which must have been at least two hundred years old, were displayed in prominent places. Exotic, animal heads mounted with various grisly expressions, all round white eyes and pointed teeth, watched him from their perches on the surrounding walls

There was more, much more, but the gloom kept some of its secrets in check. suddenly the professor felt not only lost, but claustrophobic. Before he could react, however, his supposed benefactor spoke, his voice reverberating throughout the limited space.

"It would seem you have an eye for precious antiquities, my dear sir." The tone and timbre of his voice had changed somehow, but Joseph was still trying to regain some sense of equilibrium. "Perhaps you will find something in my humble shop with which you can make friends."

For the first time Joseph saw his host clearly. The man appeared to be in his seventies, but he could also be much younger or much older. His hair was stark white and flowed straight back, almost reaching his shoulders. The lines in his face were deep and spoke of dark, well-kept secrets.

"Make friends," Lineberger said. "That's quite an interesting way of putting it."

The shopkeeper shifted his position and cocked his head ever so slightly. Just enough to capture the full attention of his guest. "You must remember, professor, these items are all representations of past eras." His arm swept outward in a grand, theatrical gesture. "They are more than just antiques. They are pieces of the past, and we can never change or control the past. Therefore, we must embrace the past; make friends with it if you will. For we can never own a piece of the past as some people so ignorantly believe. We are little more than caretakers. Guardians of the relics of history."

As he spoke, Joseph Lineberger's companion rested his hands on his knees and leaned forward. He was now gazing directly into Lineberger's eyes, and it was the old man's eyes that caught Joseph's attention and held it. They were a dark gray, almost black, and there was no luster to them at all. Just a dull gray that threatened to suck you in and suck you dry. Just like a leech.

"So, professor? Would you like to see more of these treasures from the past? Perhaps take a part of the past home with you?"

The professor's head began to swim, and he shook it enough to bring himself back to reality. "Oh no," he replied as the room began to settle, "I am sure that I couldn't even begin to afford..."

"Ah my good professor," the old one chuckled mirthlessly, "don't be too quick to count yourself out. You might be able to afford more than you think." With that the old man was out of his chair, and once again Joseph Lineberger was being propelled to another part of the store.

They came to an ornate mahogany desk with a large inlaid leather panel in the center for writing, and one smaller such panel in the top left and right-hand corners. The panels were edged in what seemed to the professor to be at least eighteen karat gold. He was transfixed by the sheer beauty of it.

The old one chuckled again. "I see you have an eye for fine things. Perhaps you would like to sit where Thomas Jefferson is said to have done some of his best work."

Joseph Lineberger blinked, his eyes owlish behind his glasses. "Gracious, mister…ah—" Things had moved so fast that the professor only now realized that he had no idea who his host was. "I'm sorry sir, but I don't believe I know your name."

The little man put his hand to his chin, thought for a second, and said, "My dear sir, I believe you are right. Please accept my humble apologies." He extended his arm, and the bewildered guest shook his warm, long-fingered hand. "I am Von Knigge. William Von Knigge. But to you dear professor, I am simply William."

"I am pleased to meet you Mr. Von…" The other man raised his eyebrows. "I mean William. I am Joseph Lineberger, but please, call me Joseph." Joseph was uneasy. His smile faltered. Something was out of place here.

There was something about this man, about this place. Something about the whole situation, and for some reason he couldn't quite fathom, he felt a sense of relief when the grip was broken. All of a sudden, it came to him.

"Excuse me, William, but I must know something."

The old man moved behind the desk. "What might that be my friend?" There was that smile again. Cold and dead. No feeling at all.

"You have called me professor, yet we have never met before to the best of my knowledge. How is that?"

Von Knigge gestured toward his reluctant companion. "Why Joseph, you have the deportment of a professor. Your clothes make a certain statement about you. Besides, there is a display of some rather fine artifacts in the museum at the university if I am not mistaken." His eyes gleamed in the near darkness. He leaned forward, across the desk. "I simply put two and two together. A gentleman of such fine character, an archaeological exhibition, one of a series of strangers in town. It all added up to professor."

Von Knigge's explanation sounded plausible. something still stirred inside the almost dry Lineberger, however. Something that would not allow him to completely lower his guard. As the professor mulled over the possibility that the old man had told the truth, Von Knigge moved deeper into dark recesses of the store.

"Stay where you are, my friend," he said from behind a heavy curtain. The curtain seemed to be a partition of some sort, closing off one part of the gloomy shop. "I have something here which I think will interest you."

Lineberger looked around the room. He could be out before the old man came back. The door was on the other side of the room, but it was not so very far. He would have to be careful, too many things to bump into and break, but he *could* make it.

He wasn't sure exactly why, but something told him he had better move while he had the chance. With a quick glance over his shoulder just to be sure, he started toward the door. He walked as quickly as he could, considering the gloom. He made it around the armor (*had this been here before?*) and by the desk (*wasn't it on the other side of the room?*) and by a floor to ceiling bookcase. On its shelves were bottles of every shape and description—every texture and hue. The centers of the bottles were dark, as if they contained shadows. In the gloom they seemed to be moving.

He paused a second to search his memory, to see if the bottles had been there before, and then thought better of it. He needed to get out. He could unravel whatever mysteries he brought out with him later.

In his haste to leave, Dr. Joseph Lineberger did the one thing that almost caused his heart to stop dead in his chest. He bumped into the bookcase.

And in his haste, he hit it hard.

In the stillness of the storefront maze, the clattering of bottles seemed loud enough to be heard on the other side of the street. Several bottles teetered and threatened to fall.

His heart hammered his rib cage relentlessly. His lungs seemed to be absolutely useless and his pulse raced as if it ran from the damned.

A long-fingered hand reached over his shoulder and steadied one large bottle full of dark shifting shadows which threatened to come crashing down in front of him.

"I see you found my collection."

Joseph gasped, his lungs immediately working again. 'Well, I…that is…"

Von Knigge smiled and exposed a double row of off-white, uneven teeth. He placed a hand on the professor's shoulder and guided him back to the desk. "I understand perfectly." There was a hint of laughter in his voice. Dark, ominous laughter. "As I said, however, I have something over here which will change your outlook completely."

Joseph was getting warmer and the atmosphere had changed subtly. Where had that bookcase come from? He knew it hadn't been there before, or at least he *thought* he knew it hadn't been there.

The closer they came to the desk the more uncomfortable he became. The room seemed a little lighter, but there was little comfort in the slight infusion of light.

"Here we are," Von Knigge said. He seated the professor on one of the red chairs in front of the desk. The chair hadn't been there before. "Professor Lineberger, I have here what may very well be the answer to your unfortunate situation."

"What situation are you—"

"*Be still.*" He held up a hand. His white hair was a luminescent mane framing an ageless face. Eyes flashing cold and malignant. "I know you Joseph Lineberger, professor of archaeology. I know you and the pitiful lot in this world like you."

The professor shrank back in the musty velvet of the chair. The combination of the thick, cloying smell of the chair and the sudden barrage threatened to take his breath away. The room was cantered at an impossible angle and the old man's face seemed to shimmer and shift. It was the same effect that pavement displayed on a very hot day. He wanted to look away, but the professor was too fascinated and too afraid terror and curiosity proving to be a powerful drug.

"Yes, professor," Von Knigge lowered his voice again. "I know you well. You who sat by quietly while your research was stolen and published under the name of another." He watched Joseph's eyes widen. "Oh yes, I know. I know about the archaeological digs. I know all about them. The major finds which you entrusted to less than honest colleagues who promptly carried them back to America and made quite a name for themselves. A name which should have been yours."

Joseph's face white. There was a greasy, rolling mass in his stomach that threatened to explode from within him. He forced back the bile which was rising in his throat. *Dear God in Heaven, how could he possibly know*?

The old man leaned closer to Joseph. "This just scratches the surface professor." There was that mirthless smile again. "Do I need to continue?"

The voice which answered in the negative was and very strained. His stomach still rolled, and sweat enveloped Joseph Lineberger's body.

Von Knigge sat down behind the desk. "There is no need to be afraid my good doctor. In fact, this may turn out to be a time of great rejoicing for you, because you are about to make the greatest find of your entire career. This find could very well change your life."

"How could you possibly have known?" Joseph was not following the conversation, his attention still on the facts this stranger should not have had access to.

"Professor." The voice was gentle. Almost soothing. "I know many things about many people. Suffice it to say that I can continue if need be. We can discuss that shrew named Minerva if absolutely necessary."

"Minerva?" For a second, he almost didn't recognize the name. Then the shock started to lessen. "You know about Minerva?"

"My God Joseph, do you need somebody to watch you every single minute?" The voice was perfect. For a moment, it could have been Minerva talking. The

old man smiled. He knew that Lineberger didn't understand the situation, but he now believed on some level. And that would suffice.

"As I was saying doctor, today you can start to regain that which should have been yours all along, and this is the item which will make it all possible."

Joseph Lineberger's attention was drawn to a cloth draped shape on the desk. With a flourish, the old man whisked away the dark cover to reveal a wooden box about eighteen inches high, nine inches wide, and six inches deep. It appeared to be hand polished oak with a latch and hinges which could have been either brass or gold. It was hard to tell in the dim light.

"Go ahead, doctor." The voice was sensual. Compelling. "Open it."

Joseph looked at Von Knigge, watched as he nodded ever so slightly, and reached toward the box. His hands moved so slow, almost as if he were pushing them through molasses.

He fumbled with the latch, stopped a moment to take a deep calming breath, and lifted the retaining pin which served the same purpose as a padlock. Once the pin was free, he opened the hasp.

The box opened book fashion. The inside of the box was covered in red satin. Cut into the left half of the box was an inset which was the same shape as the object itself. It served to hold the object in place when the box was closed. On the right side of the box was the treasure. Though it was not particularly ornate, the cup which rested snugly in the twin inset held a strange attraction for professor Lineberger. By this time, professional curiosity had taken the place of his fear.

"It's a marvelous piece," the professor observed. "May I?" He gestured toward the cup.

"By all means. Examine it to your heart's content."

The professor looked up. "Do you have a pair of gloves?"

Von Knigge laughed. "Professor, you are a man accustomed to handling things from the past. I trust you to be careful. And on this piece, I am most certainly not worried about fingerprints."

The professor nodded, picked up the cup, and held it up to better catch the light. He looked closely at the carving. Looked at the bottom, at the inside of the cup, looked at the few gemstones scattered throughout the muted gold. Nothing that could be considered ornate, but there was an elegant simplicity yet a great power in the design. The professor turned the cup over again and once again looked closely at the base. There was one mark, but not a maker's mark. Something else entirely.

"Is this what I think it is?" The professor's hand trembled slightly.

"What do you see?"

The professor looked closer, removed his cell phone, and used the flashlight function to illuminate the bottom of the cup. He studied the mark another moment, then turned his attention to some engraving on the band circling the base of the cup.

"It appears to be the mark of the Order of the Dragon."

Von Knigge smiled and stepped back. "You are exactly correct. And what of the engraving?"

"It says Vlad III, son of the Dragon."

"Very good," the old man said. So, take it to its logical conclusion. What does that mean?"

"Well, if memory serves, 'the son of the dragon' or *Dracul* is the Slavonic genitive form of Dracula. And if that is correct, that means this cup was presented to Vlad Tepes, Vlad III, when he joined the order." He looked up expectantly at Von Knigge.

"Excellent my good professor. Excellent."

Joseph Lineberger held the cup at arm's length and looked at it with something just short of reverence. "So that means I am holding..." the professor looked up, his eyes shining in the gloom.

"You are holding the grail presented to Count Dracula upon his acceptance into the Order of the Dragon." Von Knigge folded his hands together and smiled, though the expression didn't quite reach his eyes. "And there is more than just the grail if you are interested."

Joseph Lineberger placed the grail next to the box and looked at the old man. "What more can there be than this? A find like this could restore my reputation. It could make the finds that were stolen from me look like a high school science class finding shark's teeth at the beach."

The old man gripped Joseph by the elbow and ushered him back to the collection of bottles as he spoke.

"Professor, suppose I tell you that the grail will show large traces of blood in the bowl when it is examined closely. More than traces actually." He released the stunned professor's elbow and faced him full on. "Suppose I provided you with the particulars on a hidden series of underground rooms connected to a certain Transylvanian castle that contain proof positive that the legends surrounding Vlad Tepes are not legends at all?"

"You mean—?"

"I mean the historical figure was more than Vlad the Impaler. He was Count Dracula just as the books and movies have portrayed him. In short, Dracula was a vampire and the rooms contain not only artifacts no one has ever seen since his 'death,' but there is also a body neither alive nor dead in a sealed chamber among the rooms."

"One of his victims?" Lineberger asked.

"Yes. And once revived, should you choose to do so, he, along with many documents and journals among the other papers you will find, will verify that Dracula was more than a legend. It will also cement your place as one of the foremost archaeologists in history."

The professor looked long and hard at the grail, then shook his head and looked at Von Knigge. The light had gone out of his eyes as if switched off at the source.

"This is all very wonderful," Joseph Lineberger said, "but I am a man of simple means and there is no way I could pull together the funds to purchase such a treasure and mount an expedition." He looked down at the floor. "I could never meet your price."

"And what is my price?" The store owner smiled, his first actual smile of their encounter. "I have not mentioned a price. So how do you know you can't meet it?" The air grew cold and the lights seemed to dim around them. Joseph became aware of a musty smell with an undertone of, something. Something familiar that he could not place.

"Come with me," Von Knigge said as he guided the professor back toward the display of ornate bottles. "I believe you will not only be able to meet my price, but will be happy to do so." They stopped in front of the shelves of bottles. "Tell me, Professor, what do you see?"

"I see about twenty shelves of bottles of various sizes and colors."

"Alright. But what do you notice about the bottles. Look closely."

The professor moved closer and examined a series of bottles without touching them. He peered from numerous angles, then stepped back and faced Von Knigge. "They seem to filled with smoke. There is something amorphous seemingly swirling around in the ones I saw."

Von Knigge nodded, obviously pleased, and urged the professor to take a closer look. "Be very careful, but pick one up and examine it the way you would any new find."

The professor selected a bluish pink bottle about twelve inches tall and shaped like an Egyptian perfume bottle. He picked it up, looked at it from all angles, then looked at his host. "It's warm."

"Indeed it is. What else do you notice?"

"It looks like glass, and almost feels like glass. But there is something…" he held the bottle for another moment, "it's almost as if the bottle is undergoing minute changes in time with the swirling inside."

"Very good indeed," Von Knigge said, pleasure now reflected in his face. "Now, put the bottle near your ear and listen."

The professor looked at him for a moment. "Listen?"

"Yes. Listen to the bottle."

The professor hesitated, put the bottle up to his ear, then almost dropped it. "My God in heaven. What is that?"

"What does it sound like?"

"It...it sounds like someone screaming." The professor paled and his hands trembled violently.

Von Knigge took the bottle from him before he could drop it, and replaced it on the shelf. "Very astute, Professor. That is the sound of a soul in torment." Von Knigge helped the professor to a nearby chair, one which Joseph Lineberger would later, when rethinking his trip to the shop, have sworn was not there. "You see," Von Knigge said, his eyes narrowing, "I am something of a collector. Some people collect rare jewels, some collect esoteric volumes on various objects. And I," he said as he gestured toward the display of bottles, their contents ever shifting and swirling, "collect souls. Some are centuries old. The one you most recently examined, only a few decades. And I am ready to expand my collection a bit more. And that's where you can be of great assistance."

Joseph Lineberger stood. "I'm afraid that's a price I cannot pay," he said as he made his way toward the front door. "I'm sorry to have bothered you." He gripped the ornate handle and tried to open the door.

The handle didn't move.

The professor tried again, this time twisting harder. The handle remained immobile. When the professor looked back over his shoulder, Von Knigge was gone. He turned back to the door and Von Knigge was at his elbow.

"How—?"

Von Knigge took him by the elbow and led Joseph back to the chair. The cold radiating from the man's grip was like a frigid electric current direct to the professor's bones.

"My good professor, you misunderstand," Von Knigge said as he settled the professor back into the chair. "I am not interested in your soul. No indeed. I have a different exchange in mind. One that will benefit us both greatly."

"Well, if not me, then who?" the professor asked, glancing back at the door through deepening shadows.

"Your wife," Von Knigge said. "Minerva."

"My wife?" The professor's eyes goggled and he drew back in the chair. "You want my wife's soul? Whatever for?"

Von Knigge stepped back and smiled a genuine smile. "What was the last thing she said before you got on the airplane to come here? Here, let me refresh your memory.

"I can't believe you're going off to stand around with your loser colleagues. I can't believe you'd rather go to some stupid conference than take me to see my sister and her family for the weekend. But no, now I have to drive all the way across town myself while you haul your do-nothing ass to some stupid college for a

bunch of boring speeches and meeting a bunch of eggheads who will forget you as soon as the conference is over. Wasting money that I wanted to use for something that's actually useful."

The voice was so uncannily accurate that the professor flinched twice during the tirade.

"What was the something useful she wanted? Oh yes. She and her sister wanted to order some of those horrid porcelain dolls that you have all over the house. The ones with the big eyes and the all-white outfits? Every outfit is solid white, including the shoes. Am I right?"

Joseph Lineberger blinked, the shock registering on his face like a surging high tide.

"Good lord, yes. Those hideous little things are all over the house. Like a bunch of albino owls playing dress up. But how can you know all that? How is something like that even possible?"

"Do you really want that explanation? Is it not enough to know that I do know that, and a lot more? I know that I am old enough that I was there at the building of the pyramids, and those dolls are some of the ugliest things I have ever seen in my existence. How you must hate walking into your own house." Von Knigge lowered his voice and leaned closer to the professor. "Or do you really hate walking into your own house because you know *she* will be there?"

Joseph Lineberger opened his mouth to speak, then closed it. Said nothing for a long time.

"What makes you think I would offer up my wife's soul for the grail and the associated items?"

"Dr. Lineberger, I believe the actual question you have is not would you do it, but would you get caught. And I can assure you, there is nothing to catch."

"So you say, but still, taking her soul. How would that change her?"

"Oh, that's easy." Von Knigge looked down, his eyes a deep, dark, burgundy. "She'd be dead."

Joseph Lineberger stared back, unable to speak. Von Knigge laughed. "My good professor, this is how it would work. You take this bottle," he said as he retrieved a bottle from his inside jacket pocket, "and hand it to her. When she opens it, the deed is automatic, although if you don't replace the stopper within thirty seconds, her soul could reenter her body. And if you think she's a shrew now, as Al Jolsen said, 'you ain't seen nothing yet.' It's really just that simple."

"But what about Minerva. How would she die?"

"The coroner will rule it as a heart attack, plain and simple."

Joseph Lineberger sat and stared at the man, if he was indeed a man, and Joseph had his doubts now. He wasn't sure when he first realized he believed Von Knigge. And he wasn't completely sure when he realized he was going to do it.

But the deal was struck, and Von Knigge gave him his instructions.

"You are due to fly back mid-afternoon tomorrow are you not?" Von Knigge asked.

"Yes."

"Then this is what you shall do. I will give you another of those horrid dolls from the back of my shop for you to give your wife as a gift. That will placate her enough so she will not start nagging from the outset. You will then take the bottle I showed you earlier and tell her that too is a gift. Tell her it is an ancient Persian perfume bottle that still has the most delicious aroma after all these centuries. She'll remove the stopper, sniff once or twice, and the deed will be done. Then you place the stoppered bottle on a shelf with other similar artifacts of yours where it will go unnoticed. Then call 9-1-1. Tell the dispatcher your wife is unresponsive. The rest will take care of itself."

"And it is really just that easy? There are no incantations or other precautions I should take?"

"No, just stopper the bottle and call the ambulance." Von Knigge crossed his arms and looked at a somewhat changed Joseph Lineberger. "I will arrive at your home at exactly 3 a.m. with the items I promised, plus an empty collection bottle."

Joseph Lineberger's eyes grew wide. "Now wait a minute. You said—"

"Hear me out. I will arrive with those items and will leave with either one empty and one occupied bottle, or I will leave with all of the promised items *and two* full collection bottles if you have not fulfilled your part of the bargain. The choice is yours."

Joseph Lineberger thought for another moment and nodded slowly. He put the collection bottle in his jacket pocket and walked through the front door and back to the conference site.

After a block or two, Joseph realized he was whistling for the first time in years.

Husks

"You're chicken if you don't," Wayne said.

Kenny McCormick's eyes never left the old shack. "You can say what you want to Wayne," he said to the bigger boy, "but I ain't about to go in the Hughes place, and that's that." He rubbed the back of his neck just above his collar and shook his head. "Uh-uh, not me."

"That's alright Chicken Little. Just because Louise Adcock did it don't mean you have to do it."

"Damn it, Wayne, you know she went during the daytime. And all she did was run up and look in the window. She didn't hardly even slow down."

Wayne grinned. "Yeah, but she's still a girl and she still went up there." He walked over and put a brotherly arm around the skinny redhead. "Besides," he said as he started walking Wayne toward the shack, "you'll never live it down if you don't do it."

Living it down didn't concern Wayne. Living through it did. He had heard the stories about the old river shack and the family that lived in it. Especially the boy.

The kids called him Jelly Head because he was supposed to have a tiny thin body, long bony arms, and a head about three sizes too big. His skin was so pale it was almost transparent, and his skull was so thin that it looked like God filled a balloon with jelly and put it on his neck for a head.

"Wayne, I told you—"

"Yeah, yeah," Wayne cut him off. "I know what you told me. But look, we're here and it's gonna be dark soon. Besides," he said as he put his lips close to Kenny's ear, "if you go in there and word gets out how brave you are, Penny Fuller might just go out behind the gym with you."

Kenny blushed at the thought, but it was thought enough to make him reconsider. Wayne smiled. "I'll tell you what." The smile widened. "I'll even go in with you."

Wayne motioned with one hand and pushed the door with the other. The door opened freely. Kenny knew he was moving, but fear held his heart in a grip of ice. "Wayne, I'm not so sure about this." His whisper seemed to echo for miles.

Wayne closed the door behind them, flicked a lighter, and the dull yellow circle created by the flame made their shadows jump and twitch like dying souls on the wall. "Wayne," Kenny whispered, his voice catching in his throat, "we're in, now let's get out of here."

"Not yet," Wayne said as he edged toward his companion. "We've got one more thing to do." Kenny felt bile rise in his throat as his shadow twitched and leaped. "Wayne, I don't need a souvenir for proof. You can be my witness that I was here."

"You've got it all wrong," the bigger shadow said. "This isn't about taking." He lit the oil lamp on the nearby bedside table and turned to watch the terrified boy. "This is about giving."

The sight hit Kenny like a sledgehammer in the gut. The floor was littered with large husks. Dozens of them. A dry crackling sound sent a thousand tiny ice pricks along his spine. He had stepped on one of the husks. He tasted bile again, bitter and hot. But this time it didn't seem to matter.

The nightmare on the cot in front of him had his full attention.

Partially covered by a filthy sheet, it was no more than three feet away from him. The tiny body was thin to the point of emaciation, and the skin on the huge head was so thin—Kenny's left leg was suddenly warm and wet—he could see the blood vessels circling the bulging eyes and the sucker-like mouth. The thing seemed to be drooling.

"His name's Dewey, and he ain't been fed in a week or so." Wayne had moved behind Kenny and pushed just hard enough for him to lose his balance. As he teetered forward, long, hard fingers shot out from beneath the sheet and pulled him forward. The sucker-mouth opened and attached itself to his chest through his shirt with a sound like a fist punching jelly. Kenny screamed and struck out at the air with both fists. But his scream was cut short as his heart was sucked out between two ribs.

•

"You're chicken if you don't," Wayne said.

Wanda Galloway's eyes never left the old shack.

A Dusting of Snow

Snow whispered across the pre-dawn sky like a secret waiting to be told. The flakes touched trees, windowpanes, the few vehicles not housed in garages and carports, and everything else that slumbered beneath the final shimmer of moon glow.

Ed Pierce stepped off the stoop of number 23 and made his way back to the milk wagon. He was the last of a dying breed, what with the advent of grocery stores and the ever-increasing new ways of bottling milk. Still, he and Priscilla made the milk run every morning, and they would continue to make their early morning rounds until they became obsolete.

He stopped long enough to pat the flank of the milk horse calmly standing in the street, waiting.

"Prissy old girl, I hate to bring you out in the cold like this, but you've got to admit, it sure is pretty this time of morning when the snow starts falling and everything's so white." He motioned toward the house he had just left.

"Remember how old Fred Burton never bothered to cut his grass 'cause he said it would just grow back in a week or two? Just sat in the back yard under that old dead apple tree, drinking beer."

The horse nodded to gain some slack in the reins. Or maybe to answer the question.

"Lord, ain't it pretty though," he said. "Fresh snow covers up a multitude of sins."

Ed climbed back in the wagon and gave the reins a gentle flick, more habit than necessity. He and Priscilla had traveled the same route for fifteen years, and the horse knew the way as well as Ed did. She had stopped in all the right places and waited for Ed to return for the vast majority of the years they had run the route.

Ed looked at the bottles on the seat beside him and made a mental note to replace the three empties from the previous house with a chocolate and two sweet milks for the next stop.

The Fosters always got chocolate milk on Friday as a treat for the kids. Poor things, he thought. When your mama and daddy both drink to the point they can't see straight on Friday night and stay lit until Sunday, I guess a little thing like chocolate milk seems like a pretty big deal.

Priscilla stopped at the little brown house with the yellow trim on her own. The sudden lack of movement brought the milkman out of his reverie.

"One chocolate and two sweet," he said to the fading moonlight and swirling flakes of winter. "Lord love 'em."

Back in the seat and on his way again. He had about two minutes before his next stop. Ed let his eyes wander over the pearlescent tableau, and his mind followed suit. The first snowfall of the year had always been special, ever since he was a kid riding in his daddy's milk wagon in Cranston.

Familiar scenes always took on a fresh, otherworldly appearance in the first snowfall. At least they did until people started tracking it up. Then it just became slush.

That was one of the reasons he loved the route; there were few people up at this time of the morning, and the world was quiet.

Like it had been reborn.

He reined Priscilla in, again out of habit, hopped off the seat and walked around to the heavy wooden door at the rear of the wagon. Mrs. Porter would want cream and butter since her son and new daughter-in-law were coming to visit. He added a dozen eggs, on the house, because Bart Porter loved his mother's cooking—especially her Italian cream cake. And she would probably want to bake one later on.

He smiled as he left the eggs, cream, butter, and the note explaining the eggs. The fact that she would probably leave a big slice of cake out for him Monday morning didn't hurt his feelings one bit.

Ed paused, reins in hand, and looked at the house across the road. A white farmhouse with a wrap-around porch and a massive concrete planter in the side yard. It was over six feet long and close to three feet wide. Always full of flowers and decorative seasonal plants.

For years the happy façade masked a less than happy reality.

For years, folks along the road turned the volume on their televisions up a little louder than normal when the yelling started. While Milton Berle, everybody's loveable Uncle Miltie, told some television prankster, "I'll kill you a million times," Al Colquitt screamed something similar at his wife, Marge.

In stolen snatches of conversation, a neighbor would offer her words of encouragement on the few occasions he let her leave the house. But mostly, they turned up the volume and turned down their hearing.

Ed shook his head as he remembered the stories passed around the glow of a pot-bellied stove at Dickens' Store. Stories about trips to out of town doctors and long stretches where Marge didn't go to town.

Stories about the night the whole situation changed. There was still a chunk of concrete missing from the planter. Missing from the place she hit a split second before the bone in her arm jutted up through her new blue sweater.

Al just walked back in the house.

Then there was the story about the sheriff's visit to the Colquitt house a couple of months later. A neighbor had called to report somebody sneaking around outside the Colquitt house. He stopped by the house late that Friday night and found Marge out in the side yard smoothing over the fresh-turned soil in the planter.

The sheriff's visit lasted about two minutes. Just long enough for him to ask if she needed any help, and on hearing that she didn't, to remind her to be careful not to let stray dogs come out and start digging up whatever she had planted.

"If you mix up some powdered mustard and an equal amount of dried, crushed red pepper, and sprinkle it all over the soil, there ain't an animal living that will get close to it. I mean, it'd be a shame for some stray to start digging everything up," he had said. Or so the story went.

Ed clucked through his back teeth and tossed the reins. He looked out behind the milk wagon as he pulled out into the road. The new snow was already starting to fill in the wagon's tracks, leaving a flat, white plain, as if the roadway was healing itself.

The first snowfall of the year had that effect on the world. Ed nodded at the thought.

Fresh snow covers up a multitude of sins.

Problem Can

Samantha Edwards looked at the math paper on her desk. Another *F.* She was usually a straight-A student, but fifth period algebra was proving to be a real bear. The grade didn't bother her that much. Grades could be fixed.

It was the teacher that bothered her.

Gretchen Haverkamp had taught math at Twin Oaks High School for as long as anybody could remember, and, as long as anybody could remember, she had been a real pain. Seemingly as wide as she was tall, Gretchen Haverkamp had a helmet of blackish-gray hair sprayed to an armor-like texture. She trundled up and down the rows, her wide hips knocking notebooks and pens to the floor with every pass. And her voice had the lyrical quality of a bull moose clearing its throat.

Samantha's father said when he had her in school, they called her "Old Fog Horn."

But the old Dutch teacher was still there, all these years later, as much a dreaded part of every student's day as she had been when she was christened, *Old Fog Horn.*

Every year, she had made it clear from the outset that there were two things she didn't tolerate: bad grades and talking in class. And this particular afternoon there was plenty of both.

"Oh man, my mom's going to kill me." Samantha looked around quickly for the source. The nasal lament came from Hubert Mumford who occupied the seat just to her left. Hubert was mostly knees and elbows, topped off by jug ears and too-large horn-rimmed glasses.

"Hubert," Samantha hissed, "shut up before old Haverblab pops an artery." The white-haired Dutch woman was famous for her tantrums. Hubert dropped a pencil between their two seats and leaned down to pick it up. "Sam, my mom is coming to pick me up after this class. If she sees this *D-* I'm going to have the worst Christmas vacation in history."

Thunder boomed from the front of the room. "Miss Edwards, you're not carrying on a conversation back there, are you?" Sam shot a hot glance toward Hubert.

"No ma'am. Hubert just dropped his pencil and asked if I saw where it rolled."

Gretchen Haverkamp looked at the two conspirators over the glasses perched on the end of her nose, made a harrumphing sound, and turned back to the chalk board. Her broad backside twitched as she wrote, and she wrote as if every letter was an attack of chalk against slate. Neither did anything to diminish the giggles and stifled laughs spreading across the room.

Samantha turned to look at Hubert. She started to fire another nasty look in his direction for almost bringing the wrath of Haverkamp down on them, but she stopped short. Hubert was on the verge of tears.

"Can you do it now?" His eyes were moist and his face was blotchy. Sam almost told him no. She didn't like to use the problem can with this many people around.

Samantha had found the can—a deep aquamarine color, about the size of a mixed nut can, complete with lid—in the woods behind her house. It had been partially buried in a patch of wild huckleberries. She dug it out because she liked the color and thought it would clean up well and look nice on her bookcase

When she placed the can on a shelf later that day, Samantha knocked a small porcelain ballerina on the floor. The fragile left arm snapped off in a particularly jagged break. Sam picked the doll up and tried to fit the arm in place, with no success. Just then her mother called her to supper. She put the ballerina in the can and ran to the table.

When she returned after supper, the doll was whole. No sign of a break. No sign of a seam where a repair had been made.

No explanation.

After some experimenting, Samantha found the can's ability to fix things was almost limitless. Broken combs, small mirrors, China cups, and shattered crystal. It could change an *F* to an *A*, and fix more complicated problems that were written on paper and placed in the can. Problems like Matthew Henry's parents whose divorce fell through when they fell in love all over again after twelve years of constant fighting.

Samantha worked her hand into the knapsack beside her desk and rummaged around until she found the problem can. She placed the test papers, hers then Hubert's, into the can at the same moment the can was snatched from her hand.

"Miss Edwards, what is the meaning of this?" Gretchen Haverkamp was beet red. "These grades have been changed."

Samantha swallowed hard and searched her brain for a response that wouldn't incur even more wrath from the jumbo-sized educator from hell.

That's when the idea struck.

She put on her best sheepish expression. "There are others under the false bottom of the can," Samantha said. "Just reach in and push on the bottom."

Hubert's face went white.

Gretchen Haverkamp reached into the can up to her wrist.

Then her elbow.

Then her shoulder.

Oddly, there was no geyser of arterial blood. No snapping bones. No tendons snapping like hyperextended rubber bands. The process was relatively quiet. And as the astonished class watched in silence, Gretchen Haverkamp was slowly pulled into the depths of the problem can.

At long last, an orthopedic oxford clad foot (it looked like a men's size 13) disappeared inside and a few seconds later, a long belching sound issued from somewhere deep within the can.

Next, a whiff of ozone.

A second staccato belch.

Problem solved.

Prometheus

"Come in."

Victor Boyle pushed the steel door open and walked into the visitation room. Once again, he was struck by the stark nature of the place. Despite someone's attempt at softening the room with pastel blue paint and tropical prints, it didn't negate the fact that the only furniture in the room was a wide metal table with two metal chairs on opposite sides, and a small desk in the corner where an observer normally sat.

Today there was a single figure in the room. Every time he came to the facility, Victor was repulsed by the figure's appearance. Just shy of eight feet tall, the creature's intellect was matched only by its hideous nature. The skin was yellow to the point of being almost translucent, pulled taught over its misshapen frame. The mouth was little more than a black line, and watery eyes peered out from beneath a high forehead, the head covered in midnight-black hair.

"The inquisitor arrives," the figure said, its voice snapping Victor out of his reverie. "When you have reacclimated yourself to this place and to my appearance, come sit down. We don't have much time."

"Oh," Victor said, moving toward the table, "it's not that—"

"Let's not lie to one another," the creature said. "I am aware of what I am. There are mirrors in this facility. And I have over one hundred and forty years of experience with your kind. So please don't insult my intelligence."

"I…I'm sorry. That wasn't my intent."

"Regardless," the creature said, "we are here, and today is our last session as you call it. So, let's begin."

Victor sat in the chair opposite the creature and put his portfolio on the table.

"You have the recorder and are ready to proceed?"

Victor removed the digital recorder from the portfolio and put the leather pouch on the floor next to his chair. At the same time, he took the opportunity to glance under the table. As with his other visits, there was a strong chain attached to an iron ring embedded in the floor in front of the chair opposite him. The chain ended in a pair of wrist shackles secured to the creature's wrists.

Victor sat up and raised the recorder to his lips.

"Session four," he said and looked at the figure across from him. "This is to be our last conversation at the subject's request." He put the recorder down and pushed it to the middle of the table. "For the record, we have covered the majority of your life, if that is the correct word, up to this point. But there are some places where the public record, if you will, is at odds with reality. And you want to address some of those areas. Is that correct?"

The creature looked at Victor, his eyes dark and cold. Lifeless. Appraising.

"Yes. Somewhat." The eyes never left his interviewer. "It started with Mary Shelley's book. She had heard the rumors and actually was said to have seen me on one of her moonlight walks. And that is possible, because she was rather accurate in her description of me. I did my best to stay hidden in the early days. I was referred to as a soulless abomination. A creature with no conscience that showed no mercy. And there is some truth in that description."

The creature paused and looked at the recorder on the table.

"But what I really was, was a creature that wanted to be left alone."

The creature stared at the digital recorder for almost a full minute before speaking again.

"I didn't ask for this life, or this existence, whatever my condition is." It looked up, eyes dark and flat. I have read everything from Shakespeare, Faust, Pythagoras, Plato, Augustine, Origen, Aquinas, Descartes, Kant, Polycarp,

Martin Luther, John Calvin, John Milton, John Wesley, Paul Tillich, Mark Twain, and John Steinbeck, to Lovecraft, Maberry, Patterson, King, Koontz, Correia, McCammon, and Rowling. Science, theology, philosophy, and literature have no common ground and no explanation and/or answer for the question of whether my state of being is life or existence. And after years of searching, studying, and thinking deeply about the question of my state of being, I have come to a conclusion."

Victor was sitting forward in his chair, oblivious to everything except the voice of the creature.

"I have concluded," it said while leaning forward, "that it is of no consequence." The black lips spread into a cold smile. "I simply am what I am." The creature leaned back, the chain clicking against the ring in the floor.

"There is nothing else like me. For good or for ill, I am a creation unto myself."

Victor shifted in his seat. "Does that fact bother you?"

"Bother me? I would have to care in order for it to bother me."

"But all that study. All the searching for the truth. To conduct such a search for decades to discover the basis for your existence and in the end to have no firm answer," Victor said incredulously, "How do you deal with the knowledge that you have no answer for your state of being?"

"That is where you miss the proverbial boat, Victor."

The interviewer flinched. It was the first time the monster had used his name.

"You see, I am completely cognizant of the basis for my existence. I was formed by a madman who scoured graveyards, gallows, and even had an associate harvest a donor or two before their allotted time on this planet was done, to provide the parts required for my creation. Then through hours of complex surgical procedures...far beyond anything his colleagues were able to accomplish at that time, I might add...I was assembled. And from a collection of parts from over twenty corpses, through an electro-chemical process, those parts were reanimated. And what you see before you is a result of the dark genius who brought me into this world."

The monster paused as if waiting for a question. There was none.

"As for my state of being, which is the real question, after all that study and thought, I did find an answer."

Victor's eyes widened. "What is it?"

"The answer is: I don't care."

"You don't care?" Victor was incredulous. "How can you not care? You searched for the answer for decades. You have scoured the works of philosophers, theologians, scientists…the most brilliant minds from across the centuries." He paused for a moment, then said, "Do you not care, or could you not find the answer?"

Something flashed in the creature's eyes. It was only there for a second, but it didn't escape Victor's notice. He moved back in his chair.

"I found the answer within the first decade. I am a soulless creature made from the cast-off parts of dead men. But the ultimate answer is only God knows my true essence. Mankind has no idea." The monster looked down and away for a long moment, then turned his attention back to the interviewer. "I suppose when I die, I will finally have the full answer. Though I imagine I know already."

"So, you do believe in God?" the interviewer said.

"I do. I also believe in His counterpart."

Victor was stunned.

"Don't look so surprised. I am in a unique position to answer at least that one question." The monster grinned, and the grotesque result made Victor want to turn and run. "Remember who…or what…you're talking to. When I was first reanimated, I was assaulted by the memories and last moments of everybody that made up whatever I am. The force of all that knowledge and all those emotions was overwhelming.

"In in the Karloff movie and in *Young Frankenstein*—and I have to admit I asked for a copy of that one simply because it is so absurd—there is a lapse between the time I was reanimated and the time I actually moved." The monster looked Victor in the eye. "For their purposes, it was suspense. But in reality, my mind was reeling. I was overwhelmed."

They sat in silence. Victor, because of the revelations and the monster, because such was his nature. After almost five minutes, Victor said, "You said earlier 'when I die.' So, you think you can die?"

"Yes. Everything dies," the creature said, it's gaze lingering on Victor.

"Do you think it will be by natural causes, or is there some potion or elixir that might cause it?"

"Why are you so interested in my death?" the creature asked. "I thought you were interested in my life."

"I don't…I didn't mean…"

The creature smiled again. "I know what you meant. So, can I die? Probably. If it happens by natural causes, it will take a long time. Many decades, if not centuries. But eventually whatever was put into motion by that initial electro-chemical spark will run its course. Unless I burn to death. I think that is still the reason I am put off by fire. Fortunately, your world has not been reliant on fire for many centuries. So, I don't feel the same trepidation I once did. And I imagine if I am dismembered and the pieces buried in scattered locations, that would probably work."

Another silence passed between them. Victor looked at the recorder.

The creature looked at Victor.

"Tell me," Victor said, "you mentioned the movies earlier. Are any of them accurate?"

The monster thought for a moment, then pointed to his neck. "Do you see any bolts?"

"No. I don't."

"There weren't any. Electricity was a big part of the equation, but instead of bolts in the neck, the doctor used two flat metal plates attached to wires. The plates were strapped to my chest. And when the lightning struck the lightning rod, the plates took the place of the terminus of a ground wire.

"Now, Karloff did get my state of mind right in the 1931 movie. Like the scene where his monster sees the little girl throwing daisies in the water. Despite the fact that I had a blast of memories and experiences from everyone who composed my body, the world was still somehow new to me. And

Karloff did an admirable job of showing that. He saw the little girl playing and did the same."

"Yeah, but a few minutes later, he killed the little girl. Is that accurate too?"

"Yes."

"Why did you kill the little girl." Victor attempted to keep the revulsion out of his voice.

"That was a mistake. I actually did come across a little girl playing near the stream. She was plucking the head off of daisies and tossing them in the stream to watch them float away." The monster closed its eyes. "She was the first person I encountered after my escape from the laboratory, and when she saw me, she handed me some of her daisies and asked if I wanted to play a game." The creature's eyes opened, devoid of expression. "I understood what she was saying, but wasn't able to form the words yet. So, I took the daisies and we took turns pulling off the heads and watching them float.

"When we were out of daisies, she asked, 'What shall we do now?' Without thinking, I picked her up. That's when she screamed."

"I put my hand over her mouth and I twisted her head off. Then, I threw it in the water to see if it would float. And when it didn't, I threw the rest of her in the creek. That was when I heard someone running through the woods, so I moved deeper into the brush and waited."

Victor could not hide his look of shock. "Good Lord in heaven. You just killed her?"

"As I said, it was a mistake. I was still playing the game. Still gaining my mental faculties. I knew her scream would alert others, but in my mind, we were still playing. But then her father arrived, and promptly threw up. Then *he* started to scream. I almost killed him too."

"So, did you have a flash of conscience because of his obvious horror and grief?"

"No," the monster said, his face grim. "I have no conscience. I just didn't want to get caught."

Victor switched off the recorder.

•

Victor picked up the recorder and paused. He put it down again. The sun was going down and the changing light coming in through the single window high up in the wall reminded Victor that the attendant would be coming soon to take the creature back to whatever place he now called home.

"Before I go, we've talked about how you learned to talk by staying with a blind man in Germany, about your love of learning, and we've talked about how you came to be here at the institute fifty years ago. Is there anything you'd like to add?"

The monster looked at him and shook his head. "You're mistaken. I don't love anything. After a certain point, the reading was just something to do. A way to pass the interminable hours until I decided I was tired of being locked up." The creature leaned forward. "And that time has come."

Victor paled and his heart rate increased substantially. But he didn't want to show fear to the creature before him. True, the attendants would run in before anything could happen if he called out. Still, this was not a being to antagonize. Before he could respond, the monster continued.

"There is something else you need to know," the creature said as it stared at Victor. "I don't think I want you to write the book you have in mind."

"What?" Victor tried to look surprised, but his growing fear was making that impossible. "What book?"

"I said, don't insult my intelligence," the creature roared. "Do you think I don't know this isn't just a research project you're working on? Do you think I'm ignorant? Doctor Grant told me about your plans an hour before you arrived."

Victor blanched. "Now that...that's not—"

"Don't," the creature cautioned. "Before you say anything else, I want you to take a minute and think about the position you're in." The creature's eyes blazed and the chain beneath the table rattled. "I know you're an investigative reporter and I know that you have an agreement with a major publisher for this book. And I know that Doctor Grant agreed to let you perpetrate this charade for a portion of the advance, which I understand is substantial."

"I can explain," Victor said, his hands raised as if to ward off the creature.

"No, you can't. You don't have time."

"Attendant," Victor yelled. "Attendant, I need to go."

"Hush," the creature whispered. In that moment, a cold hand in a slick rubber glove gripped Victor's heart and squeezed. He could only stare in horror as the monster continued. "For an investigative reporter, you don't pay very close attention. For example, did you notice that I told you to come in, and not the attendant at the desk? And did you notice that there have been no announcements over the intercom? No footsteps in the hall like there certainly would be in a place like this? Did you notice any of that?"

Victor looked around the room and stopped when he saw the desk in the corner.

And the hand just visible protruding from behind a corner of the desk.

He turned to face the monster, unable to move. His bladder was barely holding.

"You see, even on a holiday shift change with a skeleton staff of eleven, there should have been some signs of life. But the lure of dollar signs blinded you to everything else."

Victor looked toward the door, calculating his odds.

"Of the eleven staff here this afternoon, do you know how many are alive?"

Victor stared at the creature, hot tears spilling down his cheeks.

"One. And since it's obvious you're not going to be much of a conversationalist now, I'll just tell you who. It's the janitor." The monster chuckled, and that was the last straw. Victor's bladder spasmed once and released. He was openly crying now, his breath coming in ragged gasps, his back pressed against the back of his chair.

"Attendant," he screamed, spittle flying toward the creature.

The monster ignored him. "You know why I let him live? When he first came to work here five years ago, he asked me if I had a name." The monster snorted a laugh. "He was the only one who ever asked me. To everybody else I was The Monster, The Creature, It, or worse. But Mary Shelley's original title of the book was *Frankenstein: The Modern Prometheus*, so I figured that name was as good as any. When I told him my supposed name, the janitor proceeded to tell me Prometheus stole fire from Zeus and gave it to humans and taught them how to use it, thinking I would find it interesting. I thought that was humorous."

"I would…would…I would have asked," Victor said, his chest hitching.

"No, you wouldn't. You didn't. But he did. And I told him after I had already killed everybody else that, because he asked, I would let him live. But he had to agree not to say anything to anyone until tomorrow, and when asked, he was to say Doctor Grant gave him the afternoon off because it is a holiday. Otherwise, I said I would visit him and his family in the night."

The creation of Doctor Frankenstein chuckled. "You know something? He thanked me as he was running for the door." The monster shook his head. "And you know something else Victor?" He raised his hands and showed the shackles still circling his wrists. "You missed this too."

The monster turned his massive hands over and the shackles fell away, never having been latched. The monster reached out with a speed that seemed impossible for a creature of its size and seized either side of Victor's head in his massive hands.

The reporter's bladder released its contents.

"The original Victor died before I had a chance to do the job myself, so I guess you'll have to do." Frankenstein's creation leaned forward and whispered, "Let's play a game."

●

Two seconds later Victor heard a snap, saw the wall behind him for one brief instant, then the world went dark.

Keeping Up with the Times

"Mr. Massey, you can go in now."

John Carr looked up as the receptionist motioned to the gentleman sitting beside him. The man, Mr. Massey he assumed, was a thin, balding, bespectacled, mouse of a man. The accountant type from the looks of him. The kind of man that got on John Carr's nerves. That type was usually frail, soft spoken, and easy to push around. Little or no good when it came to closing a deal.

As if sensing John's impatience, the mouse man turned and said, "I'll only be a moment."

John Carr flashed his best used car salesman smile. "Hey, hey, take your time. I'm not in a hurry." He turned the smile toward the receptionist before burying it in the magazine he had been pretending to read for the last fifteen minutes. The truth be told, he had already wasted more time than he wanted to in the outer office of Solutions Inc., and the fact that he wasn't completely convinced being there was a good idea in the first place didn't help at all.

Two weeks earlier he had no idea Solutions Inc. even existed. Had it not been for a chance meeting with Michael LoCastro, that same moment would have found him in his corner office at Ramsey and Carr, trying to figure a way to buy out his partner Kenneth Ramsey.

Kenneth Ramsey was a business dinosaur who fought progress tooth and nail. It had taken John almost a year to convince the senior partner to computerize the office.

"We're a consulting firm Johnny," he had said. "Why do we need to clutter up the offices with those things? We have a perfectly capable secretary."

Kenneth Ramsey was an old fossil. A stupid old fossil. And it was time for the old fossil to retire.

So, a little less than two weeks earlier in a pub called Linden's, John Carr saw Michael LoCastro for the first time in almost five years. And Michael looked good. That prosperous, life is amazing, kind of good.

"Michael?" he had said tentatively. "Michael LoCastro?"

The man, now he was sure it was Michael, turned, smiled, and extended his hand. "John Carr, how the hell are you?"

After a little small talk, John moved to Michael's table and they began to catch up on five years' worth of odds and ends. Marriages, divorces, old acquaintances, and other such things that time ultimately changes for better or worse. Finally, over dessert, John asked the big question.

"Michael, no offense, but what happened to you?" John gestured to a passing waiter and instantly his cup was filled.

"How do you mean?" Something in Michael's voice intimated that the question was not completely unexpected.

"Well, you've lost about fifty pounds for starters. You're wearing a Brioni suit and a Panerai Luminor watch." John shook his head and smiled. "Man, that suit and watch alone cost more than most of the cars out there in the parking lot. And unless I miss my guess, junior partners in a law firm don't make that kind of money."

Michael LoCastro looked at the watch and smiled. "That's true." He turned his attention back to John. "As for what happened, let's not talk about it here." He motioned for the check. "Let's go back to the office and I'll tell you all about it."

The Corvette his new old friend was driving was just more evidence that something extraordinary had happened to his friend. It was new.

Loaded.

And expensive.

When they arrived at the Kenworth Building, the most expensive high-rise in the city, Michael's office was just one more luxurious indication that there was a much better life out there. It was the size of his and Kenneth's offices together. And the view of the city was beyond spectacular.

"Holy shit. Would you look at this." John walked around the mahogany, brass, and marble while his friend watched approvingly. "Man, you have hit the mother lode." His words trailed off as he examined the small Picasso sketch framed and hanging on the wall.

Michael put his hand on John's shoulder, nodded, and said, "I think you're ready. Let's talk."

Michael told of his struggle to make it as a junior partner, told of getting stuck with cases nobody else wanted. He was a good lawyer. A fair lawyer. He just didn't come from the right family. So, he put two and two together and figured out that he would always be the one who handled "those cases" unless he did something. And soon.

He told John how a chance meeting with an old client for whom he had done the groundwork that resulted in a massive settlement, none of which he received credit for, sent him to Solutions Inc. The client said it was not fair that Michael had done the work and his bosses had taken all the credit. So he made the appropriate introductions, and six weeks later, Michael was made a full partner. The rest, as they say, was history.

Visions of mahogany and brass faded into the background as the receptionist's voice pulled John back into the outer office.

"Mr. Carr, you can go in now."

John Carr put away the magazine, dealt with the last of his second thoughts, and walked toward the open office door. Once again, the used car salesman smile radiated the sincerity he had practiced so long to project when it suited him. He directed it once more to the woman behind the desk, nodding his thanks, and stepped into the inner office.

The contrast was staggering.

Where the outer office was warm pine and dark leather, the inner office was a stark white. The walls were white, the carpet was white, and the furniture was white with black chrome trim. It was both bright and antiseptic at the same time.

Interesting and bizarre.

The petite woman behind the desk stood and extended her hand as John approached the desk.

"Mr. Carr, my name is Lillian Cantrell. Owner and president of Solutions, Inc." He shook her hand. Something in the cold firm grip stopped him in his tracks. His gut tightened. The salesman smile faltered a bit as he returned her greeting.

She motioned toward one of two white and chrome chairs across the desk from her own. "Please have a seat."

While John settled himself, Lillian Cantrell adjusted the computer screen on her desk and continued. "Now Mr. Carr, let me double check the information you provided on your introductory form, and then we'll get down to business."

John nodded. "Sure thing. My time is your time."

Lillian looked up. "Yes, you could say that," she said, and returned to the task at hand.

Satisfied, she pressed the enter key with a well-manicured finger and turned her attention to John Carr. The screen winked and the word *MERGE* appeared, followed by a single question mark, followed by a button for Yes and one for No.

"Mr. Carr, here are the facts. I have a very select client list, and I guarantee one hundred percent satisfaction, or you don't pay. My business is finding solutions to seemingly impossible problems, and I will do so within twenty-four hours or my services are free." She paused to let John take in the information. Before he could speak, she continued. "That, Mr. Carr, is the whole deal. If we come to an agreement, you sign a contract and I expect payment in full when the service has been rendered. Otherwise I will be forced to execute the collection clause in your contract."

Now we get down to the nitty gritty, John thought. Negotiations. This was like Br'er Rabbit being thrown in the briar patch. For the first time all morning, he felt comfortable.

John leaned back slightly and said, "Ms. Cantrell, that all sounds good on the surface, but you don't even know why I'm here. How do you know you can—"?

She cut him off. "You want to find a way to be made a partner so you can: One, take the company to new heights; and two, live the kind of life such a substantial change in position would provide. You also want your current boss to retire so, as you put it, 'the old dinosaur will finally be out of the picture.'" She leaned back slightly. "Does that about cover it?"

He was stunned. Forget-to-breathe, slack-jawed, stunned.

"What?" His mind raced. There was no way she could have possibly known that much. Nobody else knew what he wanted.

Nobody except...

"Oh, I get it. Michael called you and told you about our meeting." He relaxed. "He must be working on commission."

"I can assure you," the dark-haired lady said, "that Mr. LoCastro has not contacted me since we completed his contract."

"Then how did you know—?"

She cut him off again. "Mr. Carr, it is my business to know. After all, I am the owner, operator, janitor, and board of directors of this company. I am, as they say, the whole enchilada. So, if I don't know, who would?"

John gestured toward the outer office. "Your secretary could have told you."

"Did you tell her? Have you told anybody?"

John stood up. "OK, I'll admit I don't know how you know. But let's be honest. If you are just a one-person operation, there is no way you could—"

"Sit down Mr. Carr."

"What?" John continued to stand, but did not move.

"I said sit." Her eyes narrowed and John Carr felt something in his insides shift.

He did as she commanded.

"Mr. Carr, I have a full schedule and therefore do not have time to mince words. The simple truth is I employ certain ancient spells and incantations to achieve my means. In short, I use witchcraft. And since a witch cannot conjure money, I have found a way to survive in this new age of technology."

"Lady, do you think I'm crazy? I don't have to sit here and listen to this bullshit." He put his hands on the chair arms and prepared to stand up. Lillian's fingers tapped a command on the keyboard, and pressed enter.

John was aware of the odor before he actually smelled it. Ozone. Or something like it. His head reeled.

"Mr. Carr, you aren't going anywhere until our business is finished. If you had bothered to read the form you filled out you would know that providing the information constituted the first part of the contract. When you signed it, you signed the contract."

John wanted to get up, but couldn't. His muscles would not respond. The air was thick. He felt like he was breathing through wet cotton. Lillian Cantrell was speaking to him in slow motion—

"...a slight prick, and the contract will be sealed. Then you can go about your business. Don't forget about your payment when services have been rendered."

•

The next thing John remembered, he was back in the office.

His office.

He blinked once, rubbed his eyes, and pressed the intercom button on his phone. "Ow," he said as he shook his hand and looked at his tender index finger. "Kelly?"

Someone knocked on his door. "Mr. Carr?"

John opened the door and stood face to face with officer Richard Johns. Over the next few minutes John learned that Kelly was in the ladies' room trying to gain her composure.

The news of Kenneth Ramsey's death had brought everything to an immediate halt. The shock throughout the office was almost palpable.

"We arrived at the scene just moments after the accident," the officer said. "Almost tore the car in half when it hit the overpass support. He had to be doing at least ninety. Probably more." Officer Johns checked his notebook. "Tell me Mr. Carr, did he always drive like that?"

John told him that Kenneth was so particular about the old Mercedes that he never drove over fifty-five. "He didn't care that he made a lot of drivers furious. Caution was the key with Kenneth. 'Never move too fast,' he said, more times than I can remember. Yeah, he babied that old car."

The telephone cut into their conversation. John picked it up and put the person calling on hold.

"That's OK, go ahead and take the call. I think I have everything I need," said officer Johns. "If you need anything, just give me a call." The policeman left his card on the desk and walked outside to give John some privacy.

John turned back to the phone.

"Mr. Carr, Lillian here. As sorry as I am to hear about your partner, I believe we need to discuss my fee. Ten thousand dollars is what we agreed on, I believe."

"Lady, if you think you're about to take advantage of some freak accident, you're nuts." John Carr squeezed the desk phone's receiver, his knuckles turning white with the effort.

"Mr. Carr, I have your name on my computer screen and am about to merge it with a very nasty spell." She paused. "I had so hoped to avoid collections. So again, are you prepared to pay for my services as contracted or not?"

"Lady, I wasn't born yesterday. And I won't be taken advantage of. Now—"

He heard the click of a computer key an instant before the pain hit. His left arm was hot glass, and the nausea hit him in an intense wave that stole his breath. His chest felt like his heart was about to rupture, its erratic beat registering in his backbone. A line of drool hung from his lower lip and every breath felt like his last.

The sheer white-hot pain dropped him to his knees.

It was also the thing that convinced him this was real.

He heard a voice coming from the phone receiver which now lay on the floor at his knees.

"Mr. Carr, I will hold the spell at bay for sixty seconds while you retrieve your cell phone. I suggest you hurry."

John Carr groaned, every movement triggering a new level of agony. He finally maneuvered his cell from his pocket and looked at the screen. It showed the Solutions Inc. app.

I am prepared to pay the sum of $10,000 for services rendered. The last four digits of the card of record are 3179. Select YES or NO.

John's hand was trembling violently, but he pounded the YES portion of the screen.

Immediately the pain stopped and his breathing and heartbeat regulated themselves in a matter of seconds. He was so relieved, it took a moment to register the voice coming from the receiver on the floor.

"Oh, you're back. Good. I was just asking if you'd like a receipt."

Worms

(co-written with my brother, Paul Smith)

"I never seen so many worms in my life."

That phrase would have seemed redundant in any other circumstance. But not tonight. Worms covered every single inch of ground for ten feet or more in every direction like a carpet of tiny fingers. All pointing and beckoning in a thousand different directions, yet consumed with the same purpose.

"Quit worrying about the dad-blasted worms," Luke said, "and hold that light still."

Moss Cooper held the flashlight with both hands, but he didn't take his eyes off the worms at his feet. "Look, maybe this don't spook you none Luke, but I gotta tell you. I'm beginning to think this ain't such a hot idea."

Luke Potter, tall and thin with a fringe of greasy black hair around his otherwise bald head, stopped working on the lock long enough to punch Moss' shoulder. "Hey, get your mind back on what you're doing and maybe we can finish up sooner and go home. I ain't exactly havin' a picnic here myself." Luke went back to work on the lock.

One good twist and he felt the big spring move and pulled the door hard. The mechanism popped and a minute later the two men were in the Harrell family mausoleum.

"Luke, I don't like this at all. I'll tell you what. I'll go back out and watch in case somebody comes this way." Moss Cooper had never backed down from a fight in his life, no matter what the odds. But tonight, he was scared. And in the dank mausoleum he could feel the worms under his feet. Could feel them become pulp under his work boots.

Luke was not particularly brave, and he had backed down from many fights in his time, but he was greedy. And everybody in town knew old man Harrell and his clan had been buried wearing their best jewelry. The gold rings and diamond necklaces alone were worth a small fortune. It seemed a shame for them to just sit there, year after year, going to waste.

"Moss," Luke said, anger edging his voice, "there ain't nobody coming out here and you know it. We've watched this place every night for three weeks, and there ain't nothin' but corpses out here. Nothin' nor nobody." He turned toward the plate marking A. J. Harrell's final resting place. "Now hand me that ratchet wrench and—"

Moss grabbed Luke's elbow. "Luke, listen."

Luke pulled away. "Listen to what. I don't hear—"

Moss cut him off again. The darkness smelled like mold and…something else. "Listen Luke. Hear that rustling?"

Luke cocked his head. Turned and stepped on a fistful of worms. "Yeah, I heard it. Listen." Luke stomped the worms at his feet. Then he grabbed Moss by the shoulders. We're walking in worms you dunce. Of course you hear noises. You're squashing worms."

"Yeah, I know," Moss said. "And that's another thing. Where did all them worms come from? Tell me that Luke. Where did all them worms come from?"

Luke shook his head. "It's been raining for a day and a half, you dope. The water flushed them out. Now give me a hand with this wrench."

Luke turned back to the six-by-six-foot door in the mausoleum behind which the Harrel Clan was buried. The center bolt which seemed to hold the bronze door in place groaned under the pressure of the wrench; the first wrench to touch the bolt since A. J. Harrell was buried there thirty years earlier. Moss and Luke loosened their grip and the bolt continued to pop and groan.

The center of the plate door bulged as the two men stood there, frozen in their tracks. The worms, a living carpet of tiny fingers, waved and beckoned. Each consumed with a single purpose.

Luke's stomach lurched and rolled an instant before the door exploded into a thousand fragments. His heart stopped a split second after he saw what destroyed the massive sheet of bronze. And after a two-foot shard of shattered bronze traveled through his heart and exited his back like an express train.

Moss was not so lucky.

The nightmare had no eyes. There were huge glistening bands of mucus circling its body, and the maw that opened not two feet away from Moss was easily four feet across. Moss whimpered once and suffocated when a tidal wave of worms gushed from the toothless mouth in a solid undulating wave.

•

"I've never seen so many worms in my life," said Chief Arthur Stone as he made his way toward the mausoleum. A uniformed policeman waved him toward the open door.

"Chief, we've got something here you need to see."

Between a Rock and...

Something happened. No one's exactly sure what it was, or just how it happened. I sure don't have any explanations, rational or otherwise. All I know is something has gone wrong.

Very wrong.

You can hear it at night. A faint hiss that comes from everywhere and nowhere, like a basketball with a slow leak, or the static you pick up on an AM radio station late at night. It doesn't happen during the day, though. Only at night.

All night.

Every night.

You know, it's funny the things you think about after the fecal matter has slammed into the proverbial oscillating unit. Last night I was sitting in the study trying not to listen to the night and I started thinking about something my mama used to say.

Mama used to talk about being caught between a rock and a hard place.

It's like the time the car insurance came due and I broke my leg on the same day. She really didn't have the money to deal with those kinds of bills all at the same time. I remember because we were just coming back from the emergency room and mama hadn't said anything for about half a mile. She just drove. Once in a while she'd glance at my brother over on the passenger seat, then she'd check the rear-view mirror and look at me stretched out on the back seat. You know, back when you could do that kind of thing without some government or societal entity blowing out a brain cell.

The dam of emotions she had been doing her best to hold back finally cracked while we were stuck at the red light on Hillcrest Street. She looked at both of us, then started grinning. A minute later the crack in the dam widened and she started chuckling. She looked at my brother, glanced in the rearview mirror to look at me, then Bob farted. And it wasn't any polite little toot. No sir. My brother Bob is a world class farter, and this was one of his best. A blue-ribbon window-rattling prize winner.

At first mama had that deer-in-the-headlights look. A sort of *when-did-the-cat-learn-to-speak-Latin* look. Then came the, um, shall we say, pungent payoff.

The light turned green, then immediately back to red.

The dam broke.

She laughed so hard we sat through two more cycles before she was able to regain her composure. When I asked her if she was alright, she started to say something but started giggling again. I put my hand on her shoulder and must have looked like an eight-year-old trying to look grown up. By this time, we were moving again and she was composing herself one last time.

"I'm fine," she said. "Really, I'm fine. I just started thinking about things and I just figured things couldn't get any worse. Then, Bob pooted and I knew things really could get worse. Then I knew we were caught between a rock and a hard place."

She grinned at my brother, and he beamed. Grinning like he'd discovered the cure for cancer and halitosis all in the same day instead of fogging up an Oldsmobile with leftover hot dog and chili fumes.

That phrase is a cliché to most folks. But it wasn't when mama said it. She said that sometimes things kind of pile up and the pressure keeps building until you find a release valve of some kind and let it go. My mama's release was laughter. The worse things got, the more she'd laugh. Sometimes she laughed at Jack Benny or Red Skelton.

If I dood it, I'll get a whippin…I'll dood it.

And sometimes she just started laughing for no reason at all. She said sometimes she just thought funny things.

But now the whole world is caught between a rock and a hard place. We're caught in a brutal place. A place we don't understand. Not like the time we fought the war to end all wars, or the handful of wars that followed it. This isn't something as simple as war. It's more like the world finally pissed off some great unknown something, and now the payback's coming.

We're caught between a rock and a hard place.

But this time, nobody's laughing.

The whole thing started about three weeks ago, not that it matters now. But that's when it started. And for the entire three weeks the pencil pushers in Washington (and everywhere else in the world) have been speculating and disagreeing about who caused it. They can't fathom the fact that, as the bumper sticker says, *shit happens.* The Pentagon authorized reconnaissance missions 'round the clock, even over our own bases, and the world's best collection of egghead scientists haven't even come close to an agreement on anything. But they all agree on what the outcome will be.

Six weeks from now at the very outside, we'll all be gone.

Every one of us.

We're caught between a rock and a hard place.

And every evening at dusk the hissing and crackling and popping starts. Every night another layer of reality is eaten away. It's like an invisible swarm of celestial locusts comes at dusk and begins eating away the next layer of the world until dawn. Something's coming, and it's taking its own sweet time about it.

All the trees are bare. It's June fifteenth but it might as well be January. There's not a leaf to be seen anywhere, and the bark on the trees is almost gone. Any exposed power, telephone, and cable lines are almost completely stripped, every brick house in town looks like it's been sandblasted. And the wooden buildings have already been so structurally compromised they're pretty well uninhabitable.

At first some of us gathered at the courthouse during the day to divide into teams and scout around town to survey the damage. You know, just in case the finger pointers and eggheads were wrong and this whatever it is somehow stopped and we could start to make repairs. Kind of like triaging patients in the emergency room.

The problem is, that started to wear thin after the first week or so. The air smelled funny–ozone coupled with something else. Something more unpleasant. And the whole outdoors felt, well, it felt different.

Alien.

Vacant.

Even with twenty or more of us standing there in sight of each other, the whole outdoors felt like what Charlton Heston was supposed to be feeling during the daytime in *The Omega Man*. But that wasn't why we called off the expeditions. *That*, we could deal with.

The thing that put an end to our expeditions (and pretty much the last of our hope) came a week ago when we started finding the animals.

Squirrels, mice, owls, dogs, cats, snakes, chipmunks, horses, cows, birds all looked like they had been flayed down to bare muscle, sinew, tissue, and bone. Stripped of fur, flesh, and feathers to varying degrees.

And all very much alive, if you call thrashing, writhing, and convulsing in agony life.

We put as many out of their misery as we could before we finally gave up. God only knows how many more are still out there. Each one spending the night in the clutches of something consuming them alive a layer at a time, and spending the day in the clutches of a body trying desperately to heal itself.

Or to die.

And in the not too distant future, so will we.

All of us.

No place to run. No place to hide. Caught between a rock and a hard place.

So, the scouting stopped. There was no discussion, no special meeting or agreement made between us. We just didn't go out again. Couldn't bear what we knew would find.

The Johnson family down at the end of the street said they are going to travel by day and stay wherever they can at night. They've got some crazy notion they're going to outrun whatever it is. At first I thought they were crazy. After all, the night still comes. And whatever is out there is still out there devouring creation one layer at a time.

But I guess even running beats just sitting and waiting for the inevitable. Caught between a rock and a hard place. In a way it's almost funny.

But this time nobody's laughing.

No, this time the joke's on us.

The days are getting shorter.

We Create Them

Myra Banks ran a well-manicured finger around the rim of the Steuben wineglass. The thin bell tone of fine crystal never failed to make her smile. She had become accustomed to the finer things in life and had what she felt to be a genuine appreciation for them. The daughter of a moderately successful hardware salesman and a dedicated but underpaid elementary schoolteacher, she decided at an early age she was going to be more than just another lower middle-class hausfrau. She was not going to scrimp and save for every little scrap the way her parents had done their whole lives.

Two years out of college she met Glenn Banks; a successful public relations company owner and her ticket out of the lower middle class she loathed. His success, coupled with his willingness to give her everything she wanted without question, made him the ideal husband. He was successful, wealthy, and most often away on business. That combination gave her more time to enjoy the lifestyle to which she had readily become accustomed without anyone's interference. And all she had to do was wear the occasional low-cut gown to company functions and provide a little sex two or three times a month.

Not a bad deal in her estimation.

In the same way she treasured things of great worth and beauty, she had little patience for things she felt were below her standards, including people.

Especially people.

"It's so refreshing to share a meal with someone who appreciates quality," she said to Pamela Wright, who smiled and said nothing. Myra had been talking for the better part of fifteen minutes; a monologue on fine art, fine restaurants, fine wines, fine cars, and fine homes. A constant barrage of trips to Aspen, the car she absolutely knew Glenn would surprise her with on her upcoming birthday, and a pending trip to New York with "the girls" for shows and shopping.

A waiter, well versed in the art of serving, poured more cabernet and retreated a discreet distance until needed again.

"As I was saying to Brenda Perkins just last Thursday, those of us who are fortunate enough to have nice things have a responsibility to uphold a certain standard." Myra sliced a portion of veal, mated it with a wine-soaked mushroom, and paused long enough to place the morsel in her mouth.

After taking the proper amount of time to chew, swallow, and wash the Veal Marsala down with the wine, she gestured, inviting her lunch companion to look around the room.

"For example, there are those who can't afford to frequent a restaurant of this caliber, but those of us who have that ability should never feel we have to justify our choice, or feel that we need to explain ourselves because we chose to live the lives we live."

Pamela placed her knife across the rim of her plate and spoke for the first time since the beginning of the main course.

"I wasn't aware you've been expected to explain your life to anyone."

Myra took a sip of wine and shook her head.

"Well, I don't mean literally explain. It's more the attitude of people I'm concerned about. The things they don't say." She gestured toward the window to her right.

Beyond the walnut and brass confines of the restaurant was Commerce Park. Little more than an abandoned lot at one time, various charities and private concerns had raised the money to landscape the parcel, put in a fountain, and construct cobblestone walkways through the area. The park was a beehive of people walking, jogging, or sitting on a bench eating their lunch as the world passed by.

At any given moment the park played host to mothers pushing babies in strollers, lovers holding hands and dreaming dreams. Businessmen took a much-needed detour on the way back from lunch while the dozen or so homeless denizens of the city watched from the fringes, occasionally trying their luck with a likely looking soul who might have some change or even a dollar to spare. An ever-changing cross section of the human race passed through the park all hours of the day and night, and it was to the current mix of humanity that Myra gestured.

The homeless ones in particular.

"How many of them would like to trade places with us right now?" Myra glanced at the platinum blonde sitting across from her, and then turned her attention back to the window. "How many of them would give anything to be sitting right here where we are? Have you ever wondered about that?"

Pamela looked at the human tableau, started to look away, and paused. A scabby face appeared in the window. The topographic map of wrinkles showed a landscape littered with despair. The dead once-green eyes flickered with something akin to recognition and the old man opened his mouth as if to speak. Pamela cocked her head slightly, the movement almost imperceptible. The old man shuddered as if waking from a dream, then shuffled out of sight. His diamond pinky ring a blunt contrast to the filthy work pants and ragged pullover sweater he wore.

She allowed her glance to linger a moment, then turned her attention back to Myra.

"I don't know that many of them actually give it much thought," Pamela said. She sipped from her water glass and continued. "My guess is most of them are just trying to survive with little or no thought as to what goes on in here." She paused, sipped water, then continued. "Sure, there are probably some who wish their lot in life was different, but those people tend to work to find a solution and better their circumstances through hard work or education. And many others are content with their circumstances."

"That's my point exactly," Myra said. They are where they are because of choices. If they took responsibility for their actions, tried to do more than simply respond to their circumstances, they would see just what life could really be. They wouldn't have to rely on just their circumstances."

Pamela's stared at her lunch companion, unbelieving. The only responsibility Myra had ever taken for her circumstances was lying on her back for a balding, paunchy executive at a conference and promising to do the same, for better or for worse, till death—or dwindling bank account—do us part. Then she let her gaze drifted back to the scene outside.

"Maybe they don't mind their circumstances. Maybe they're accustomed to their lives to the point that the rest of it really doesn't matter." She turned her attention back to Myra. "Maybe they know deep down they will never have this kind of life and it really doesn't bother them."

"How could it not?" Myra asked, her voice incredulous. "How could you know what the alternatives are and not want something better? How could you possibly be satisfied with less if you have the ability to create a better life?"

"Create a better life or have better things?" The smallest hint of a smile formed on Pamela's lips at her companion's look of confusion. "Don't you really mean how can they do without all the things you have?" She shook her head. "Myra, you seem to forget that the quality of life is not judged by the quality of the things you have."

"Well of course it isn't, but you have to admit that having is much better than doing without. I should know. I come from a family of have nots, and I swore I would never have to live the way my parents did. I swore I would find a way to do more than just get by." She took another sip of wine and gestured around the room. "And here I am."

Pamela looked out the window and watched an old woman walking toward them. The frail, slightly stooped husk of a woman shuffled down the sidewalk, her hair a mass of tangles. Her teeth stained a dark mahogany by snuff and neglect.

Myra followed Pamela's gaze and shuddered. "That's what I'm talking about. Look at her." The words were filled with venom. She stared as the old woman made her way toward the restaurant, and made no effort to hide her disdain as she drew near.

"How in the world could someone allow themselves to come to that?" Myra asked no one in particular. "Just look at her. It's disgusting."

Pamela's platinum hair framed a face gone hard; a silver-white cloud from which the beginnings of a storm threatened.

"What are you saying?" Pamela's eyes, the center of the storm, narrowed imperceptibly. "What makes you think she had a choice in the matter? What makes you think she wasn't just like you at some point in her life?"

"Like me?" Myra laughed. "She and I have absolutely nothing in common." She looked at the old woman and shuddered. "Absolutely nothing."

The woman stopped in front of the window beside them and looked in. Her nose, ravaged by the advanced stage of melanoma, pressed on the glass. A thick, clear liquid seeped around the edges of a ragged scab. Wisps of hair, a mottled, rat-colored gray, moved in the breeze. Dirty spider webs drifting on unseen currents.

Her clothes were a curious mix of Salvation Army and thrift shop cast-offs. But one thing in particular drew Myra's attention.

Her shoes.

The handmade Italian shoes easily cost twenty-five hundred dollars. The quality was undeniable. Such beauty had no place on the feet of someone so pathetic.

Pamela saw that the shoes had captivated her lunch companion. "Myra, sometimes the choices that lead them to their lives are different than you imagine. In fact, you two have more in common than you think. That old woman could just as easily be you."

The words hit her with the force of a cold slap.

"Me?" She said the word as if hearing her voice for the first time. "The only thing she has worth having is that pair of shoes, and heaven only knows where she got them. She probably stole them. Those people are born that way. They are born with a penchant for stealing."

Lightning flashed in narrowing platinum-framed eyes.

"No, she wasn't born that way. Nobody is born that way," Pamela said, her face darkening. "Look at her." Something in the air spit and crackled. "Take a good look."

The old woman still stood at the window. Silent and unmoving, a monument to all things wretched.

Myra shook her head and closed her eyes as if to will the woman away. When she opened them, nothing had changed. And once again her gaze was drawn to the Christian Louboutin pumps. As she looked, unable to stop staring at the old woman, she was vaguely aware of Pamela's voice, a winter draft that bared its teeth and bit at something deep within her.

"Look at her, Myra. Look beyond the dirt. Beyond the filthy clothes, the sores, and the grubby fingers. Look into her eyes."

The room darkened, and though the woman before her was repulsive in a way she would never be able to describe, Myra was helpless to look away from what must have once been pretty eyes. Eyes that once saw shapes in the clouds and colors in rainbows after a summer rain.

Eyes that were now empty. Eyes that had lost their sparkle, and something much deeper. Dead eyes, the doorway to a dead soul.

"We create them, Myra. They are not born that way. Those who walk the streets in endless days of frustration and despair are never born that way. We create them. One by one. Each in his or her own time.

"In almost everyone you meet there is the potential to become one of these seemingly aimless ones. So many people live the illusion of a good life, yet just beneath the surface, they are little more than avatars of those like her." She pointed to the face in the window, her gaze never leaving Myra's face.

"The truth is, we create them. We suck the life out of them until there is little of the person they once thought they were. We feed on them. We feed on the false life they radiate. We take the shallow ones, the ones like you, and we strip them of their arrogance. Their outward trappings. We reveal their true essence.

"We feed on the lie that is their so-called life."

The voice mellowed and the room swam back into focus. Myra was startled to find the old woman was gone, though she could smell her, the essence of her, through the glass.

She felt dirty.

Myra grabbed for her wine glass, all sense of decorum gone for the moment, and drank as if the act of drinking would banish the memory.

The waiter appeared again and started to pour. A slender finger touched the back of the waiter's hand, and a blue-white spark jumped. The waiter stopped pouring and stood still. "We will have the check now," Pamela said. The storm inside her was subsiding for the moment. The waiter nodded and produced a pastel card covered with the practiced strokes of one accustomed to writing down the whims of others. He placed the check on the table and moved his hand before the white-maned woman could touch him again.

Myra took the check with an unsteady hand. Her companion made no move to stop her. Instead, she watched as Myra produced an antique fountain pen and a platinum credit card. A nervous laugh slipped from between Myra's quivering lips.

"Society can't be responsible for what I just saw," Myra said as the waiter walked toward the kitchen and the waiting credit card reader. "There are too many places set up to help people like that if they really want it, and too many people like me...

She hesitated.

Started to speak.

Stopped again.

"...like us...who give to charity so people can help themselves." Her voice gained a bit of strength. The waiter returned and waited for her to complete the transaction. Though her hand still shook she signed the receipt, the platinum of the card somehow soothing.

Pamela stood and walked. Myra followed. They went behind the door marked WOMEN.

Myra blinked. Rubbed her forehead. "Pamela, I just don't believe society is responsible for people like that. I can't believe it. Society is people; people like you and me, and we do our part. We..."

"That's where you're right," said the woman standing in front of her. It was Pamela, but not Pamela. The platinum hair shimmered and undulated as if possessed by a will of its own. "We do our part. You and I. But I never said *society* creates them.

"Didn't you notice anything familiar about the woman in the window? Anything at all?" The air was getting heavier by degrees. Time moved slowly, and Myra watched as the platinum entity spoke. Its skin began to ripple and change, becoming translucent. The air shimmered and the woman who was once Pamela began to shimmer as well.

Platinum and mercury.

Life and death.

Yin and Yang.

Heaven and hell.

Myra tried to shake her head, tried to speak, but the effort required to do so was beyond her. She felt so...

"...empty," the voice continued. "That's the similarity. You're so obsessed with the trappings of life that you have never experienced life itself. You waste life. Discard its goodness like a rancid banana peel. You are little more on the inside than a dried-up husk bedecked in garish colors, your existence little more than a faux life."

Myra felt tired. Bone weary. Washed out. So much so that the quicksilver being of light that had once been her dinner companion was little more than a distraction. It was true. She didn't care. She just wanted to go away. To be left alone.

But the talon fingers—were they fingers, she didn't know anymore, didn't care—gripping her shoulders found purchase and held her fast. She felt herself being lifted. The tile floor was now at least four feet below her. And for the last time in her life, or maybe the first, Myra Banks *felt* something.

We create them.

Myra felt herself losing the will to live. Felt herself growing weary. Tired. Old.

The silver giant sighed, its mouth stretched wide in an effort to catch every drop of faux life before it could be wasted.

Creating.

•

The old woman stopped at the window and watched the man seated at the table inside. His white-maned companion stared at him intently, mostly listening, sometimes speaking, and always watching.

Infinitely hungry.

The quicksilver woman on the other side of the window pointed toward her, the old woman, the old woman in the shapeless housedress and filthy sneakers. The old woman whose once yellow-gold hair had begun to come out in clumps.

She watched as the quicksilver woman said something to the man. He seemed not to hear, seemed to be in some sort of trance. He got up and followed the quicksilver woman when she motioned.

After a moment, the street dweller shuffled down the sidewalk, her antique pen clutched to her chest.

A Rustle of Owls' Wings

I hear them mostly at night. Mostly when I sleep.

Sleeping.

Waking.

Sometimes I'm not sure which is which.

But I know I hear them.

The owls.

I hear them mostly at night.

I first heard them when I was a child. I dreamed about the owls. The owls with the big eyes. Staring. Probing. Watching me. Evaluating. Questioning. Talking without making a sound. Never a sound.

I remember how I used to sit in the dark, afraid to go to sleep. That's when I would hear them. Them and their rustling blue-gray wings. They were all blue-gray. The owls who spoke without speaking.

I remember I used to sit in the dark and wait for the sunlight. I prayed for the sunlight, but there was always darkness. Always too much darkness, and the big-eyed, soundless owls.

They asked me questions. Big questions. Questions I didn't understand then and don't fully understand now. Questions about where I came from and how I got here. I'm from here and I've always been here. I don't understand what they mean.

I've always been here.

And the owls have always been here. They have sailed the silver-black skies as long as there has been a sky to sail. Theirs is the whole universe and they will take wing at will and span time and space.

They say they are somewhat like us.

But they don't understand.

The first time I saw the owls clearly, I was six. I had caught glimpses of them, seen them through the haze before that, but the Christmas when I was six was the first time I really saw them.

We were at my grandma's house, had spent Christmas eve there; and though I loved Grandma Templeton better than almost anybody in the world, I couldn't help wondering how Santa Claus would ever find me. I hadn't told him in my letter that I was going to be gone. And once I realized my mistake, I was afraid he would either leave all my toys at our house—and I would have to wait three days to see them—or find no one home and just take them all back to the North Pole until next year.

But mama said he would always be able to find me. He always knows how to find you wherever you are.

Somehow, that thought didn't comfort me.

But Christmas eve turned into Christmas day and Santa did indeed find me. Then Christmas day turned into Christmas night. And the house, so recently filled with light and the sounds of carols and the smell of cider and evergreen boughs, turned dark and still and cold.

And they found me. They have their ways.

At first, I sensed them more than saw them. I was asleep in the attic room of Grandma Templeton's big Victorian house. Over the years that huge room had been the lookout tower of a great castle, a rocket to the moon, Superman's Fortress of Solitude, and the site of a hundred more little boy fantasies. But that night those fantasies were lost forever. That night I felt something that shouldn't have been there—something that shouldn't be, period—and shuddered myself awake from a sound sleep.

I rubbed my eyes and looked around the room. The forms around me took vague shape in the dim light of the moon. I saw the rocking chair in one corner, and the faint image of the small Christmas tree against the far wall. I saw the dresser and the toy box right there where they had been for years. Everything exactly as it should be. Everything exactly as it had always been. But nothing was right. The night was wrong. The lights were wrong. The light of the moon and the dust motes that swam down its lunar stream were wrong.

As I lay there listening with every nerve in my body wide open to the slightest sound, straining to catch even the most minute change in the air, the chair in the corner started to rock. Slowly at first, then faster. Back and forth and back and forth. *Cree, thumpa. Cree, thumpa.* Faster and faster and back and forth until I knew it just had to tumble over and slide across the room. And all the time the chair—possessed with a manic life of its own—was rocking, the lights of the tree began to glow. Not all at once, but gradually. Like some unseen hand was slowly turning up a rheostat.

Without warning, the electric train began to travel around the base of the Christmas tree. Smoke poured from the stack, the headlight flashed, pistons advanced and retreated, while the wheels clattered on the track at breakneck speed. *Clackity, clackity, clackity, clack, clack. Clackity, clackity, clackity, clack, clack.* Train and tree, carefully unplugged hours before, glowed and clattered while the rocker in the corner continued its frenzied dance.

I wanted to scream. To call out for help. But I couldn't. I couldn't speak. I couldn't move. I could only watch in a combination of mute fascination and abject terror as the other occupants of the room, inanimate until a moment earlier, mutinied against the laws of science and sense.

Clackity, clackity, clackity, clack, clack. Cree, thumpa, cree, thumpa. Clackity, clackity, thumpa. Clackity, clackity, cree, thumpa.

I wondered why nobody heard. I wondered why my rescuers weren't already running up the stairs, rushing in to pull me from the confines of my animated prison, and rush me to safety. I looked down and willed my legs to move, to kick away the covers and carry me to safety, but they wouldn't move. They were as useless as if I had been paralyzed since birth.

My chest and throat burned with the effort of trying to make myself heard. A great internal pressure brushed against my rib cage and I felt like my lungs would burst any second.

You have nothing to fear from us.

The voice came from all around me.

You are safe.

More a thought than an actual voice. I didn't hear it so much as I was aware of it. Like someone else was thinking my thoughts for me. I tried my legs again without success.

Why do you struggle?

Even then the grand absurdity of the question was laughable, not that I felt the least bit like laughing then, or now. How could they not know I was terrified? Couldn't they understand I was just a little boy? And even though I tried to make the questions come out, tried to make them go away, the sensual onslaught continued.

The questions continued as did the reassurances. But I didn't want reassurance. I wanted them out of my room and out of my head. I wanted to wake up and find the train still, the tree dark, and the rocker sitting quietly in its place. But the train still whizzed around the track, teetering and smoking on every curve, the tree flashed in time to the thrumming of the train, and the already frenzied chair had increased its tempo.

Then, as quickly as it started, it stopped. Train, chair, and tree all ceased their macabre rondelet and went back to their previous inanimate existence as if nothing out of the ordinary had happened. In less than an instant they went from whirling dervish to deadly still.

Why are you afraid?

The large black eyes of the one speaking—I don't know how I knew that was the one. I just knew—were the last thing I saw before I passed out. The pressure in my lungs and the pressure in my mind needed a safety valve, and unconsciousness was blissful release.

The rest of my memory of that night comes in bits and pieces. Flashes of coherence in the midst of insanity. I can remember a large gray room with a table or stretcher or some other such thing in the middle of it. The owls were all standing around the table. Standing and staring. Watching. And the walls; the walls seem to be moving in and out ever so slightly. I felt like I was inside something alive. Something breathing. In and out. In and out. Rippling and flexing. In and out.

All the while there were voices. The whole time I drifted between consciousness and oblivion, there were the constant voices. Voices that made no sound.

What are you?

...walls moving...breathing.

We must see...

eyes...

is in place and intact...

voices with no sound. Pain. I need...

It is time to return...

The next morning found me in bed, Roy Rogers pajamas and bed covers rumpled, but no more than unusual. I didn't remember anything beyond the time I first crawled into bed. I was nauseous until about noon and didn't have much to say—too much excitement was Grandma Templeton's diagnosis—but there was no memory of anything other than going to sleep. Mama and daddy packed up the car, and I packed up my memories. Buried them deep.

Thirty years deep.

I know I have seen the owl since then. I remember bits and pieces. I remember seeing the lights. And although I have never been to Texas, I can tell you what the Corpus Christi skyline looks like reflected in the water.

I remember vast expanses of black, dotted with silver-white light.

I've been studying the owls. Learning what I can without having too many people look at me like I have a third eye.

I used to be afraid of the owls. Afraid of what they might do to me...

the pain

Afraid of what they have to say. But I'm not so afraid anymore. Not so much. Because I've found others like me. Others who have seen things.

Others who have feelings they can't explain and time for which they can't account. They haven't all seen owls—some can't remember just what it was they have seen—but they remember the eyes.

And together we remember bits and pieces. Some have seen the room with the table, and some have seen other things.

But we all remember the eyes.

And we all remember what it was like trying to explain to everybody we care about that our lives didn't seem to be our own anymore. We remember the eyes of our wives and husbands; the faces of our children. That's another memory we'd like to forget.

But even those things don't seem so important anymore. Because for some reason the memories of the owls have been coming in larger bits and pieces. And when I wake up fast enough, or write my thoughts down quick enough, I can make out more of what the owls were saying. Are saying. Not all of it, but more than before.

I've always been here.

And they've always been here.

The owls with the big black eyes. Eyes that watch and probe. Eyes as black as a bottomless pit. But I've started to remember. And I've seen their pitch-black eyes up close. They're empty, haunting eyes.

Empty, but not vacant.

Not by a long shot. The owls know things. There is the wisdom of the ages in those eyes.

They have always been here. They have always been everywhere. This universe is their domain. Every universe is their domain.

And they are coming back. Soon. I don't know how I know, but I know it as well as I know my own name. And this time when they come, I'm going to remember it all. The sights, the sounds, the smells. I'm going to remember every last detail.

They may have been back many times, but I wasn't ready. They said so. They told me in my head and in my heart. But this time I am ready.

And I know they're coming back.

The sun is setting. Night is falling. And before long, they'll come for me. The blue-gray owls who speak without speaking.

I am going to sail the boundless reaches of time and space. The universe will be mine.

And just before we make the last transition and I stand poised on the edge of infinity, I'm going to look back on who and what I was before the owls came. I'm going to watch as the memory fades into the distance, and listen with a new understanding. And I am going to sail the silver-black sky as long as there is a sky to sail.

I will not be back.

Croatoan

The Lost Colony.

I know what happened to them. Harris Faulkner just confirmed it.

But I'm afraid the confirmation comes too late.

•

First things first. I'm a community college history professor with a Master's degree in American History. I am nothing special in that regard. I teach at a small community college on the North Carolina coast. Or rather, I used to. The Human Relations Department and the academic dean have been calling, texting, and emailing almost non-stop for a week. At first my lack of response probably worried them because I'm one of those faculty members always referred to as solid. Dependable.

"You can always count on Michael Beck," they'd say. "Michael is so dependable. Let's add him to the Planning Institutional Effectiveness and Accreditation Committee. He'll make a solid member."

The word they use when I'm not around is *boring.* And what they really say among themselves is most likely "Let's add him to the Planning Institutional Effectiveness and Accreditation Committee. He's boring as hell and he'll probably think it's some kind of honor."

After a week of trying to find me with no success they probably sent me a warning letter.

If the college is there next week, they'll probably send me a termination letter.

Que será será.

The fact of the matter is, I *am* boring. I don't go out much. I don't have a wife and kids. I don't even have a dog. It's just my books and me. And for a man in his mid-forties a lot of folks no doubt think I'm a bit of an odd duck. Seldom going out. No steady girl.

Do you call them girls or women when you're in your forties these days? I'm not sure. Then again, I suppose it doesn't matter now since I don't have one. Haven't had one for a long time.

Like I said, it's just my books, my research, and me. And for years that has been enough.

I have done enough research on my own to qualify for a PhD twice over, but finances and circumstances long ago put such a thing out of reach. Then again, that doesn't matter at this point. I know what I know, and the fact that I don't have another advanced degree on the wall is not going to change the outcome of this narrative one iota.

I'm recording this from a luxury resort in Jackson Hole, Wyoming. I'm using a digital recorder because my hands are shaking, and my handwriting is hard enough to read on a normal day. So this will make things easier for whoever finds the recording.

That is, if anyone ever *does* find it.

OK. Back to Jackson Hole. It's an incredibly nice place. My room runs about eight hundred dollars a night, and I've been here for about a week and a half. I have eaten most of my meals in the three-star restaurant just off the lobby, and I've also taken a cab over to the Hilton and had drinks and the best steak ever produced by a cow at Westbank Grill.

Twice.

It's the kind of place where, if you have to ask how much something costs, you probably can't afford it. But I'm not worried about paying the American Express bill next month, partially because the card I'm using isn't mine. It belongs to a fellow historian who blew his brains out just before I came out here.

Right after I told him what I knew.

Three weeks ago taking advantage of a situation like that would have been unthinkable. Reprehensible. But now? Well, it doesn't really matter. Not anymore. And that's because of the other reason. The one that could make this recording an exercise in futility.

I don't think we will be here much longer. We will all suffer the same fate as the Lost Colony and a dozen other groups throughout history.

[One Minute and Forty Second Pause]

So, what do I know that you don't? That requires a brief history lesson.

In the late 1500s, the English made their first attempts to settle in North America. Sir Walter Raleigh sent 120 settlers to establish a colony on behalf of Queen Elizabeth I. The trip from England to the New World took three months. The settlers arrived on Roanoke Island, one of the barrier islands located just off the coast of North Carolina, on July 4, 1584, and soon established relationships with two native tribes, the Secotans and the Croatoans. But by April of 1586, many of the settlers returned to England because of a shortage of food and a series of Indian attacks.

On July 22, 1587, John White and one hundred fifteen new colonists returned to try and establish a second colony in the area. Their first act after landing was to check on the previous colony. To their surprise, they found nothing except a skeleton that may have been the remains of one of the English garrisons. Still, they formed a second colony on Roanoke Island. Later that year, John White, the leader of the colony, headed back to England to get more supplies. During that trip a major naval war broke out between England and Spain. Queen Elizabeth I immediately called on every available ship to confront the Spanish armada. So it would be three long years before John White would be able to return to the colony, his wife, his daughter, and his granddaughter, Virginia Dare, the first English child born in the colonies.

When he returned in 1590, the settlement was deserted. The settlers had mysteriously disappeared. The only clue he found was the word "Croatoan" carved in a tree. Croatoan was the name of an island south of Roanoke that was home to a Native American tribe of the same name. The same tribe the settlers with whom the previous colony had established a relationship.

Investigations into the fate of the "Lost Colony" of Roanoke have continued over the centuries, but no one has come up with a satisfactory answer.

Until now.

But before I got to the point—yes, I really will. But I have to do it my way, as Frank Sinatra so eloquently said—it's important that you know about some similar incidents.

In December of 1872 the crew of the British brig Dei Gratia saw an American merchant brigantine, the Mary Celeste, drifting erratically about six miles away. Both ships were approximately 400 miles from the Azores at the time. After observing the floundering vessel for a while, Captain David Morehouse ordered his crew to change course in order to offer assistance in case the American ship was indeed in trouble.

When the captain and some of his crew boarded the Mary Celeste, they were amazed by what they found. One of two pumps had been disassembled and the only lifeboat was gone. There was at least a six-month supply of food and water on board in addition to a completely intact cargo of alcohol. The ship's captain, his wife and daughter, and the crew were all missing. The sails were in poor condition and the rigging was heavily damaged with many of the ropes hanging over the side of the ship. The forward hold was closed, but oddly enough, the aft and lazarette holds near the pilothouse were open.

It's interesting to note that in the early days of shipbuilding, lazarette holds were where the bodies of important passengers who died onboard were stored until they could be returned to the family. Passengers of lesser financial stature were just buried at sea. The only explanation modern-day technology has been able to provide is that the events occurred because the ship's inhabitants fled for some unknown reason, and evidently in the process of trying to escape, the lifeboat capsized.

The bodies were never recovered.

To tell the truth, I'm not sure they ever made it to the lifeboat, nor do I think there were any bodies to recover.

Next, we have the story of the six hundred inhabitants of the town of Hoer Verde, Brazil. In 1923, a group of visitors came to the village and the first thing they noticed was that the village was strangely silent. Hanging signs swung in the breeze and the subsequent creaking could be heard, but otherwise there was no sound. There were no people moving about either in the lanes or in their homes or businesses.

Local law enforcement was called in and during their investigation they found a gun at the town's school. In addition, they found the words *There is no salvation* written on the blackboard. A massive effort to find the six hundred inhabitants turned up nothing. None of the villagers were ever found. The official report concluded that the town's inhabitants seemed to be "gone without a trace."

Let that one sink in for a minute.

And finally, let's consider the case of the fishing village on Lake Anjikuni in Canada. Normally the village was home to between two thousand and three thousand Inuit settlers. However, in November of 1930 when a fur trapper named Joe Labelle returned to the village after a trapping expedition, there was no one there. Just like the village of Hoer Verde, every man, woman, and child was just "gone without a trace." Every shack was empty, but there was nothing missing. All of their food, supplies, and weapons were just where they should have been.

The Royal Canadian Mounted Police conducted a thorough investigation, and in addition to the lack of inhabitants, they found all the bodies of the dead had been removed from their graves. And as if that wasn't enough, all of the sled dogs were dead from starvation and buried beneath snowdrifts. Now in a land where your life could easily depend on having a dog team, no villager in his right mind would have left without his dogs. They were simply too valuable as both companionship and transportation.

The only thing the RCMP learned during their investigation was that nearby settlers had seen strange objects and lights in the sky just days before the villagers disappeared.

UFOs maybe?

We should be so lucky.

[Two Minute and Thirty Second Pause]

So, what does a collection of historical mysteries have to do with The Lost Colony other than being one of a dozen or so similar historical anomalies? And moreover, what does any of it have to do with us?

That's the part that no one will believe. Well, that's not exactly true. Dr. Eugene Timberlake, formerly of Harrison University, believed me. So much so that he painted the wall of his study with his brains when I convinced him that there's one more such incident on the way. Probably the last one. And I'm pretty sure it will be on such a massive a scale that it will make this recording a waste of time. In fact, after what I just saw on television, I'm almost sure of it. But I've come this far, and I'm racking up a bill I could never hope to pay without a dead man's American Express card, so what do I have to lose? I'll tell you what I know and what I think I know. And if there's anybody here to listen to this later on, then you be the judge.

As I said in the beginning, I know what happened to The Lost Colony. And it was the similarity between that event and the others I've described that lead me to look closely at the source documents and other historical documents associated with the various disappearances. And in looking, I noticed a number of additional similarities that have been overlooked over the years. Overlooked or just plain ignored. Some were in the form of direct evidence and others came via stories and alleged events passed along by witnesses to the events.

Let's start with the colony. In addition to the stories and books we are all familiar with, there are a set of stones called the Dare Stones. The stones are supposed to have been written by Eleanor White Dare. She was the mother of Virginia Dare, the first child of English descent born in the colony. The first stone, supposedly inscribed by Eleanor, was found in 1937. By 1940, forty-seven additional stones had been found, all of which purported to tell the ultimate fate of the colonists. A stone dated 1592 indicated that the survivors made their way to the Nacoochee Valley area. Another stone dated 1598 told of Eleanor's marriage to the tribe's king, and another told of the tribe's anger when she gave the king a son. They demanded that the infant be sent back to England. A stone dated the next year told of Eleanor's death and the daughter she left behind. And it's a good story. But there are three problems.

Problem one: Dare Stone number one is most likely authentic, but the others not only can't be authenticated, but are universally thought to be forgeries. The presence of drill press marks and the non-Elizabethan language are a dead giveaway.

Problem two: The stone no one talks about. The flat one with four words engraved on it: *The King in Yellow.*

The stone's authenticity is not in doubt. In fact, scholars of the day were so sure of its authenticity they locked it away. Only certain academics were told of its existence and a relative handful were ever given access to it. Because in addition to the four words, there were a series of symbols carved around the outer edge of the stone. Symbols unlike anything scholars, researchers, and iconographers had ever seen before

Problem three: Martin Van Hoek. The world's most self-aggrandizing geologist.

For a while in the early 90s, Martin Van Hoek was the rock star of the geology world. I know, that's a bad joke. It's also a lot like saying he was the tallest of the seven dwarfs. But to give the devil his due, his finds were not insignificant. First, he located one of the largest veins of gem-quality emerald in history just outside Franklin, North Carolina. Two years later he discovered a massive gold field in Alaska. The resulting sale of the rights alone was enough to provide a lifetime income for every member of the village under which it was found. And his swan song a year later was his uncovering the location of massive coal reserves in an area of Great Britain thought to be mined out. The discovery led to both a reinvigoration of the economy and the establishment of thousands of coal mining jobs once thought to be lost for good.

Again, all good things.

For the next few years, Van Hoek was featured on every scientific journal cover remotely related to the field of geology or any of the other natural sciences. He even made the cover of *People* for the North Carolina emerald find. Thanks to him, a lot of celebrity fingers and cleavage would be on display bearing the fruit of his labors. And after the Great Britain coal find, he was touted from one end of the realm to another as the savior of the village of Elbermarle. And all was well as long as he was able to accept speaking engagements, party invitations, testimonial events, and interview requests.

But, as the cliché goes, all good things must come to an end, and thus it was with Martin Van Hoek.

The accolades waned, the parties and testimonials dried up, and the few articles that dribbled in were little more than filler for more important stories. His long-winded answers to simple questions posed for sidebar pieces were cut to a mere sentence or two here and went unused. And that was… wait, I need to hear this.

[Five Minute Pause]

Dammit Harris, that's not what I wanted to hear. But unfortunately, you're the only one who seems to have a clue. You're the only one with enough sense to call in an expert in something other than sound bite speculation and at least get the fact that this is not a terrorist attack on the air. Everybody else seems to be taking the easy way out. Talking about everything from dirty bombs to EMPs.

But you, Harris Faulkner, just looked at the evidence, maybe did a little research beyond the normal, and then took the bull by the horns. And from the expression on your face, I have a feeling you just made a giant leap in logic that will make most of your colleagues shake their heads in disbelief and most news directors choke on their coffee.

Oh shit.

Enough of talking to the TV.

What the intrepid Ms. Faulkner just realized is that this story will turn out to be unlike anything she has ever covered. And all the standard bets are off. She has spent the last fifteen minutes showing footage relayed from a helicopter flying over Innsmouth, Massachusetts. For the last fifteen minutes there have been real-time images of deserted streets, abandoned buildings, cars idling in driveways, a few cars even overturned in ditches, and an eerie silence punctuated by the droning of the copter's blades.

No cats, no dogs, no curtains moving in the window where someone tries not to be caught looking. There is just a town. And not a living soul to be seen.

Then came the sound. It started as a low guttural thrumming then became an ear-shattering wet, growling, grating sound unlike anything I have ever heard in my life. Then…nothing.

No helicopter.

No pilot's commentary.

No video feed.

Nothing.

Just Harris live on the air, static hissing and popping where a live feed should have been, saying what I've been feeling.

"Oh shit."

Girl, you don't know the half of it.

[Two Minute and Fifteen Second Pause]

The residents of Innsmouth, Massachusetts are gone. Just like the pilot who was looking for them. Just like the people of Kingsport, Massachusetts a little farther down the coast. Just like the Lost Colony and all the other missing people I told you about earlier. They were a series of appetizers, if you will. Maybe a brief appeasement much like sacrificing virgins to the volcano gods in those campy 1950s science fiction movies. But this time I don't think anybody will write about them. Thanks to the incredibly vain Martin "Don't-Forget-About-Me" Van Hoek, I think we are all truly and royally screwed.

The main course is about to be served.

You see, when Martin realized the limelight was officially shining on someone other than him, he did the only thing he could think of. He went to the scene of his previous triumphs and started researching. That's the funny thing about geology. The right conditions always produce results. For example, put carbon under enough pressure and it produces diamonds. Not sapphires. Not quartz. Just diamonds. Certain conditions produce emeralds, others produce rubies, and so on. Sort of like two parts hydrogen and one part oxygen makes water. But sometimes the process by which those things happen should be heeded. And sometimes the hazardous conditions surrounding some geological finds should be enough to tell you to move on and keep looking.

But Martin wasn't hoping to benefit anyone with any subsequent discovery other than himself. He was hoping to find another dose of Andy Warhol's coveted fifteen minutes of fame. To his credit (giving the devil his due and all that), Martin had a knack for going to places where deposits were thought to be tapped out and finding additional deposits. And he did it through single-minded research and advanced scientific testing.

But like many who are only in it for themselves, he only paid attention to the parts that had a direct bearing on his project.

He ignored the history surrounding the research.

While retracing his steps in North Carolina, he learned of an old all but forgotten tale. Or if not forgotten, seldom spoken of. As the story is told, after the Lost Colony disappeared, a group of Croatoan Indians brought a massive obelisk all the way from their island to the mountains near what is now Cherokee, North Carolina. The coastal tribe received permission from the Cherokee nation to bury it, with the caveat that nothing could be done on Cherokee land. They did not want their ground tainted. But they would allow the Croatoans to do what they had to do nearby so the object could be watched.

The Croatoans agreed and set to work.

The obelisk was nine feet tall, four feet in diameter, and was made of a substance that looked and shone like obsidian. But the surface had a slick, oily feel. And while not reflective—in fact, it seemed to "swallow the light" as one tale recounts—if one stared at it long enough, it is said they would begin to see things. Indescribable acts of violence and cruelty. Hideous creatures. Things that defied description.

The obelisk had been hidden in a cave on their island for centuries until one of the visiting settlers found it and a group of them brought it out of its resting place. The Croatoans objected, but the colonists saw their objections as little more than ignorant superstition and they took the obelisk back to their settlement with the intent of sending it back to England in exchange for additional supplies.

The obelisk never left for England.

At least not then.

After the colony disappeared, the Indians retrieved the obelisk and made their decision to remove it from their island that very night. Throughout the subsequent journey they kept the obelisk wrapped in animal hides and blankets and tied securely. Once they arrived in the mountains, two of their most skilled artisans spent the better part of a day splitting the obelisk into three sections while a medicine man chanted and the rest of the party prepared a burial place.

The carvers could only work for about an hour at a time. One, because the substance was hard to cut, and two, because after about an hour, those tasked with splitting the obelisk would begin to feel sick and start talking to no one in particular. Sometimes they spoke in a language none of their brothers understood. So they would work on the object and rest.

Early the next morning the obelisk lay in three long pieces on the ground. One piece they buried on the spot, still wrapped in animal hide and blankets woven with holy symbols throughout the design. The other two they wrapped in similar hides and woven blankets also covered in holy symbols. Then they set out to find a certain trapper whom the Cherokee medicine man knew they could trust.

They found John LaPatrie down by the river loading his canoe. Once they explained their purpose and the fact that they had been sent by the Cherokee medicine man, LaPatrie listened to their story silently. Never questioning them. Never so much as nodding. He sat on the side of his canoe as silent as the stone at their feet. When the medicine man finished, he too fell silent. All seven men looked at the trapper. After a full minute one of the artisans said, "We do not expect you to do this thing without recompense. We have brought…"

LaPatrie quieted him with an upraised hand, looked down at the two wrapped stones, then slowly shook his head. The tribal chief's son, leader of the group, spoke up. "Sir, do not turn us away. Large River of the Cherokee tribe says you are a man of great understanding and great honor. Please…"

"No," LaPatrie broke in. "I am not refusing you. I just do not want those things near me." He looked up at the men before him. "I have seen lights that have no source. Heard sounds that have no human voice. I have seen the forms of comrades long dead coming to me in the night. And for everything I cannot explain, I have heard even more tales from men I know to be honorable and sober. Men of both the land and sea have chilled my blood with tales of things that cannot possibly exist, yet still do.

"So yes, I will help you. But no. I want no compensation. All I ask is that you help me build another canoe. A bigger canoe that I may pull along behind me. I will put your damned objects in that one, deliver them to two seamen I know, and tell them your tale. They will take the objects far from here and do just as you have done.

"Then I will set fire to the second canoe and scatter the ashes."

They all agreed and set to work. Two days later the canoe was carved and loaded with its obscene cargo. Before he set off, the chief's son asked again, "Can we not give you at least a part of the pelts and beadwork we brought for such a purpose? You are doing our people a great service."

The trapper shook his head. "Some things are diminished by payment. How can I profit from your misery and still call myself a man?" He watched them for a moment and continued. "However, if you have one of those blankets left, I would be pleased to have one for my own protection. I admit I will be uneasy until those things are gone."

The men conferred among themselves and one of the artisans spoke. "All of the sacred blankets are wrapped around the objects, and we don't dare remove even one. But wait one moment." He fished in a pouch on his side and brought out a large piece of amethyst. "We found much of this stone while we were digging the burial pit. Wait for a few moments please." With that the two artisans began working the dark purple stone. One held while the other fashioned a rough shape. Then one began refining the shape while the second man began stringing small colorful stone beads on a thin ribbon of hemp. Twenty minutes later the men presented the trapper with an amethyst cross to wear around his neck.

"I believe this is the symbol of your Christian God," the medicine man said. "It is our hope that it will protect you as our holy symbols might have done."

The trapper nodded, shook hands with each of the Croatoans, and launched the canoes. At this point I could relate the story of each fragment and how it came to be in its final resting place. But I think time is running out, and I have some special plans for later tonight. So suffice it to say that the trapper was as good as his word. He found the two seafarers he had hoped to find, relayed the Croatoans' story, and asked for their help. The captains agreed to help under the condition that LaPatrie arrange to have the fragments loaded himself. The captains and both crews said they would only lay hands on the pieces of the obelisk long enough to take them off the ship and bury them.

So, the trapper agreed. He hired four men to load the fragments on the two ships, paid them with the last of the money he had, then went to a dark place beside the seawall and, using the sharp edge of the amethyst cross, cut his own throat. Much like the Croatoan men had done after he launched the two canoes. Only in their case they returned to the spot where they had buried the first fragment. The two artisans killed the others in their group with the axes they had used to cleave the obelisk, and then turned the axes on themselves.

The captains and their respective crews didn't fare much better. The first captain and his crew were sailing north on the Emily Anne, and the first part of the journey was uneventful. But as they neared the end of their journey, a freak storm blew them off course and the ship wrecked off the coast of what is now Canada. There were no survivors. Years later bits of the wreckage, a few log books, and the obelisk fragment were given to a small Maritime Museum in Maine where they stayed on display for over a hundred years. Then, through a case of misidentification, the fragment was "identified" as Inuit and in a grand ceremony the fragment was presented to the Inuit people. Its last known home was the community lodge in a small fishing village.

A small fishing village on Lake Anjikuni in Canada.

The second ship suffered a similar fate. The Mary Beauregard set sail to return to England with a hold full of spices and fruit and vegetable seeds. But their trip was considerably longer than that of the Emily Anne, and by the second month, the captain had begun acting strangely and giving unusual orders. And his punishments for the least offensive infractions were often cruel and swift. On one occasion, just because a member of the crew questioned his order to throw all the surplus rope and sailcloth overboard, he demanded a pair of pliers. When they were brought to him, he clamped the crewmember's tongue with them and cut it out.

As the men began siding with and against the captain, things became even more intense. There was talk of mutiny, and a confrontation between the captain and his first mate became an all-out brawl. In less than half an hour every crewman lay dead, most disemboweled or hacked until they were almost unrecognizable. With no one at the helm, the ship floundered far off course and ran aground in the Azores.

Quite a coincidence, huh?

Wait. Hold on a minute.

[Twelve Minute Pause]

Harris, you're starting to get on my nerves now. No. That's not exactly true. You're starting to scare the hell out of me. And you just pushed my timetable up.

A lot.

[Two Minute Pause]

OK, it's time to wrap this up. I'm not going to be here much longer. When I said, "Quite a coincidence" earlier, I was talking about the fragments of the obelisk turning up at sites where there have been mass disappearances. But that's just the beginning of the end. At each of those sites there was another "coincidence" linking them together. In each case a man in tattered yellow clothing was seen at the site. His features were indistinguishable, but the clothes made an impression. In the case of our trapper friend, the constable's report indicated "a man in yellow clothes, tattered and worn, was seen in the crowd surrounding the deceased man, but moments later he was nowhere to be found." And the story of the murder/suicide at the burial site told by the Cherokee includes the sighting of a white man with a very white face and ragged yellow clothes walking away from the site as tribal members went to check on their coastal visitors.

The same figure seen at Hoer Verde and near Lake Anjikuni just before those disappearances.

And just now he showed up in the news footage from the California coast.

That's the other thing Harris has been reporting on. There has evidently been a slight shift of the tectonic plates in the Pacific Ocean. The shift has affected oceanic patterns from California to Pearl Harbor and well past the coast of Japan. I find it interesting that she's working that story *and* the Innsmouth story. I'm betting she has an inkling of what I know. Maybe she knows about Martin Van Hoek too.

And no, I didn't forget our friend Martin. Oh no. That self-aggrandizing son-of-a-bitch is the cause of everything that is about to happen. Because in his rush to find another feather for his cap, his research uncovered the story of the three parts of the obelisk. So, he tracked them down, collected them, and brought all three pieces to one particular location to begin a nationwide tour. His plan was to make it a mobile touring historical display, much like the Vietnam Traveling Memorial Wall.

So, he brought the pieces to the starting point of his great traveling ego tour, *joined the pieces together again*, and prepared to bask in the applause of the crowds once more.

But the history he planned to highlight was the wrong history, because the obelisk is older than history. It is not an object to be observed. It is more of a celestial tuning fork. It was designed to do something more than point the way to the past. When the stars are aligned and the obelisk is whole, it will awaken the first in a legion of terrors we cannot hope to comprehend. The obelisk's *only* purpose is to waken Cthulhu, who currently lies "dead but dreaming" in the submerged city of R'lyeh. And where is this submerged city? It's somewhere deep in the Southeast Pacific Ocean.

According to the Pnakotic Manuscripts, one of the most ancient texts on the planet, when the stars are perfectly aligned, R'lyeh will rise from beneath the sea, and Cthulhu, the first of the Great Old Ones, will awaken and devastate the earth.

And the herald of these events is Hastur. No one knows its true form. It has no definition. It is simply a floating mass with tentacles and suckers, much like an octopus, and it will devour everything in its path. But it is often seen in some semblance of human form wearing tattered yellow clothes and a mask to hide its true features.

Hastur.

The King In Yellow.

Cthulhu's half-brother.

The same form I saw in the background of the plate tectonics story from California. A figure in tattered yellow clothes with a nondescript face standing just beyond the crowd gathered at the shore. A figure that will be there when R'lyeh rises and the end begins. The same figure who was very likely there in the crowd when Martin Van Hoek unveiled his traveling doom show.

In Innsmouth, Massachusetts.

[Twenty Minute Pause]

OK, I think I have said everything I need to say. I finally had to turn the TV off. There is a lot of excitement on the west coast. But in the immortal words of Al Jolson, "You ain't seen nothing yet." Maybe they will be the lucky ones. The first to go. Who knows?

All I know is I have the last thousand dollars in cash I'll ever see in my pocket. In about fifteen minutes, a young lady named Tracy from a reputable (does it really matter now?) escort service will knock on my door and we will take a cab to the Westbank Grill for the best steak ever produced by a cow. Then we will take a room at the Hilton and I am going to get as much of my thousand dollars' worth of Tracy's services as I possibly can. We may just talk. We may do other things. I don't know. But when we are through, I am going to use two more bullets from Dr. Eugene Timberlake's Taurus 9mm pistol.

One for her and one for me.

And while she won't know it, I will be giving her the most valuable gift anyone has ever given her.

Because despite the fact that I am almost a thousand miles from the California coast, I have begun to smell the tang of the sea on the air. And just beneath the tang of the sea, there is something else.

I believe it is the smell of death.

I will leave you now.

May God have mercy on our souls.

[Twelve Hour Pause. *Overpowering Thrumming*]

*ph'nglui mglw'**nafh** Cthulhu **R**'lyeh **wgah**'nagl fhtagn...ph'nglui mglw'**nafh** Cthulhu **R**'lyeh **wgah**'nagl fhtagn...ph'nglui mglw'**nafh** Cthulhu **R**'lyeh **wgah**'nagl fhtagn...*

Bad Place Alone

The first limousine arrived at 10:00 in the morning. Four identical automobiles arrived, one every twenty minutes, until the last Rolls Royce Limousine Phantom arrived at 11:20 and deposited its bewildered passenger.

Benny Taglio stood in the circular driveway and stared up at the house in disbelief. The royal style residence, an elegant merging of Baroque and Rococo architecture, was easily more than 60,000 square feet. But that, along with the mansion's striking contrast to its surroundings, was lost on Benny. The grounds surrounding the opulent home appeared to be miles of cracked red clay spotted with sharp, needle-like limestone pinnacles emerging from the ground, and camelthorn trees giving the appearance of skeletal hands reaching to the sky.

Benny, however, only saw that he had been dropped off at some big-ass house and his ride just drove off and left him without a word. To make matters worse, he had no idea when the driver was coming back.

"Mr. Taglio, come in. We've been waiting for you."

Benny looked up and saw the double front doors were open. The owner of the voice was a short, squat little man dressed in what looked like a Giorgio Armani tuxedo. Benny looked down at his own Armani track suit and Berluti slip-ons, shrugged, and walked up the front steps.

"Hey, Jeeves," he said to the short, tuxedoed figure, "maybe you can tell me something. Where am I, and where did my friggin' driver go? This is highly irregular."

The little man rubbed his hands together. "Those are all interesting questions Mr. Taglio. And they actually go straight to the heart of the matter. So, if you'll just come in, freshen up from your trip, and avail yourself of the amenities, all will be revealed in good time."

"Yeah, but—"

"I said, all in good time." The voice cut the air like a scalpel. "Now come in and get ready." There was no humor in the face above the immaculately tied bow tie. The eyes were cold and unblinking. And something in that look told Benny it would be in his best interest to do as he was told.

Now.

"Yeah, OK," Benny said as he walked through the doorway. "I didn't mean no disrespect. This is all just kinda unusual, you know what I mean? What with being invited to some house I've never been to before by somebody I don't even know."

"Indeed, I do," the little man said, a modicum of good humor returning to his voice. "And I can assure you, things are about to get very interesting. So, come in and meet the rest of your group."

As Benny walked into the house, his escort placed a hand in the small of his back to usher him in. The hand was cold and Benny felt the chill as if the hand had pressed ice into his bare back. Benny increased his pace and heard a snicker as he stepped into a black marble hallway. The walls were lined with hundreds of niches, each of which housed a painting and information plaque, illuminated by a dim, unseen light source. And while his tuxedoed escort was walking ahead of him at a very brisk pace, Benny registered the titles of a few paintings.

"The Nightmare," by Henry Fuseli; "Judith Beheading Holofernes," by Caravaggio, and a painting of the same name by Artemisia Gentileschi; "Saturn Devouring His Son," by Francisco Goya; "The Garden of Earthly Delights," by Hieronymus Bosch; "The Face of War," by Salvador Dali. And there were at least a hundred more equally as macabre. They were nothing like he'd ever seen before, or wanted to see again.

"Jeez, whoever owns this joint's got some weird taste in art. Why not just get a dozen or so paintings by that famous Italian guy? You know...Bott something."

"The famous Italian guy, as you so charmingly put it, is Sandro Botticelli, and his paintings would not fit in with the rest of the decor," the small man said, never looking back or breaking stride. "These paintings have all been selected for their power and their portrayal of the ultimate truth of human life." He paused in front of a set of large black ironwood doors. "Here we are," he said as he opened the door on the left. Solid and just short of twelve feet tall, the door weighed in excess of one thousand pounds. Yet Benny's escort opened it with ease. "Please go in and mingle. Your host will join you within the hour." His escort smiled, an expression that didn't spread to his eyes, and motioned toward the room beyond.

Benny stepped into what appeared to be a library. The sound of the door closing echoed like a cannon shot.

He stood for a moment and stared. There were floor to ceiling bookcases on every wall, each one containing hundreds of books. At regular intervals there were reading tables with a banker's lamp and two chairs. Closer to the entrance was a series of five leather wingback chairs, each with a side table. The tables rested on a pair of Zieglar Mahal Persian carpets, any one of which would have sold at auction in excess of one hundred and fifty thousand dollars.

"Ah, the latest arrival. Do you have any idea what is happening, sir? Any idea why we're all here?"

The question came from a fifty-something banker-type in a tailored suit. His small, thin mustache twitched as he spoke. Three other people flanked him. One was a young man in dirty jeans, and a tee shirt advertising some band Benny had never heard of. He had a thin, hatchet face, dirty blonde hair, and some faint blonde fuzz desperately trying to be a chin beard. Next to him, filling a glass from a bottle of amber liquid, was a woman in a red and blue tennis skirt and top. Her blonde hair was offset by a blue visor. She glanced toward Benny and turned back to the bottle. The final guest, a tall woman in a long red evening gown, slit high and cut low, sat in a leather chair near a small side table. She held a drink and raised it in greeting when Benny looked her way.

Each guest looked expectantly at Benny.

"Me? No. I don't know nothing. I was hoping one of you might know what's going on." He walked a little closer to the group. "How about you, blondie?" he said to the woman in the tennis outfit. "You got any idea why we're here?"

The blonde woman in the visor stiffened, then crossed the distance between them with the grace of a cheetah, and towered over him. Her voice was cold, and the slight tremor could have been either fear or anger. "First, my name is Carol. Not Blondie. And no, neither I nor anybody else in this room knows why we're here. If we did, we wouldn't have asked you if you knew, now would we? So, do you have any other questions we don't know the answer to or are you done?"

Benny blinked and held his arms out wide. "Geez lady, I'm just making conversation here. This is all highly irregular."

"Well you at least got that much right," Carol said and returned to her original spot near what appeared to be a fully stocked bar. Carved mahogany with brass accents, and easily fifteen feet long, it looked small in the room by comparison.

"You might as well hit the bar and wait for the other shoe to drop," said the woman in the red dress. "If your trip was anything like ours, the driver just dropped you off and left. So basically, we've just been milling around here trying to kill time until we find out what this is all about."

"OK," Benny said. "I think I get all that. So let me ask you this, if that's OK," he said and looked at Carol. She shrugged and went back to her drink. "Have any of you ever been here before, or ever heard of this place before?"

"Not me," said the boy in the band tee shirt. "This the strangest damn place I've ever seen."

The man in the three-piece suit nodded in agreement. "I think we would all agree that this place is completely unfamiliar to us. It remains as mysterious to us as the reason we are here, whatever that is."

Benny thought for a moment, then started walking around the room. He paused every dozen steps or so and ran his finger along the spine of a book or picked up one of the many small statues that rested on various shelves. He read some of the titles aloud. *The Victorian Book of the Dead*; *The*

Empire of Death: A Cultural History of Ossuaries and Charnel Houses; *Wonders of the Invisible World: Being an Account of the Tryals of Several Witches, Lately Executed in New-England*; *The Necronomicon.*

"What the hell is this crap?" Benny put the last book back on the shelf and wiped his hands on his pants. "That thing even feels creepy."

"Well, if it really is the Necronomicon," said the young man with the anemic beard, "then it's bound in human skin."

The group stared at him in disbelief.

"What?" he said. "Just because I come from a trailer park doesn't mean I can't read."

His companions continued to stare. The man in the suit broke the silence. "Are you serious? What kind of book is bound in human skin? Honestly."

"All I know is it's also known as The Book of the Dead and was written by some mad Arab named Abdul Alhazred. It's a book of spells and dark magic. It also has a history of The Old Ones and tells how to summon them. H. P. Lovecraft wrote about it a few times in his stories."

"Even so, human skin? Are you certain?"

"Well how about you go grab it and see how long you can hold it before your balls want to go back where they came from?" Benny said and wiped his hands on his pants again. "Listen," he said and gave one final wipe, "I know you're probably tired of hearing this, but I'd really like to know what's going on here." The woman in the tennis outfit opened her mouth and Benny held up a hand. "Yeah, yeah, I know you don't know anything about what's going on here. So, let me ask you this. What kind of land deal are you expecting when our *host*," he said as he made air quotes, "finally shows up?"

"Well, I for one am not here for land," said the woman in the red dress. "I am here to negotiate a major business deal."

Benny nodded and looked at the young man who had just schooled them on the Necronomicon. "Ok buddy, how about you?"

The young man rummaged behind the bar and found a beer. "Hey, whadaya know?" He held it up for everyone to see. "It's my brand." He popped the top and took a long drink. "I needed that. I'm getting kinda warm." He pointed the beer can at Benny. "And the name's not Buddy. It's Doug. And I'm not here about no land. I'm a mechanic, and this guy wants me to keep up his old cars. He's evidently got forty-five or fifty of 'em. Really sweet rides like Mustangs, Porsches, and Bentleys."

"OK," Benny said and turned his attention to the man in the suit. "What's your story?"

The man in the suit took a breath, held it for a moment, then let it out in an almost inaudible sigh. "My name is Stuart Burton the third, and I am here at the behest of our benefactor to avail myself of an investment which, if I am approved, could double my net worth in thirty days." He shot his cuffs and sniffed. "So, I doubt I am here for any kind of land deal. But since you brought it up, who are you and why are *you* here?"

"Fair enough," benny said. "I'm Benny Taglio from New Jersey and I'm here to take advantage of a sweetheart land deal. Some property so remote nobody else wants it. But I have some uses for it and I'm here to make the deal."

Benny turned his attention to the woman in the red dress.

"OK," she said before Benny could ask her a question, "let's go ahead and get this over with. My name is Tiffany Thorne. I work as a hostess at the Bellagio in Las Thornes, and I am here to work out a deal that will eventually make me a co-owner of the newest hotel in Thornes." She turned to look at Carol. "And for the sake of getting this over with, Carol, why are you here?"

Carol folded her arms over her chest, looked at her companions, and shook her head.

"I won the lottery."

Tiffany snickered. "Carol honey, considering what I do for a living, I think I can say without fear of contradiction, we have been, or are about to be, royally screwed."

Benny headed for the bar. After making himself a drink, he walked over next to Tiffany. "Lady, I do believe you are right. I find it hard to believe we were all called out here for different reasons by the same person. So given what we know now, how do we find out who brought us all out here, and why?"

"I believe I can help you with that."

Benny dropped his drink and spun around, his hands groping in his pockets and coming up empty. The others, equally startled, looked toward the now open doors through which Benny had entered earlier.

The same squat man in the expensive tuxedo who escorted Benny in now stood in the doorway, backlit by an unseen light source. "Ladies and gentlemen, if you will follow me into the dining room, all will be made clear."

•

The table around which they sat was easily large enough for twenty people. The massive room had English oak walls and the windows behind them were decorated with deep red velvet draperies. Above the hand polished oak table were a pair of massive bronze chandeliers.

They all sat on one side of the table facing a wall on which hung an ornate gold mirror, easily nine feet by twelve feet. There was no other furniture nor any pictures or other decorations on the wall. Just the mirror.

"Ladies and gentlemen, I know you have many questions at this point. And I promise every one of them will be answered. What I will tell you now is that you were all hand selected and your arrival at this place is no accident. Each of you were carefully considered, contacted, and brought here based on your talents and your history.

"Again, the full story will be revealed for each of you very shortly. But I know you must be hungry after the long day you've had so far. So that being said," he snapped his fingers and two doors opened behind them. "Dinner is served."

"Thank goodness for that," Carol said. "I feel like I've already been here a week."

Servers dressed in attire similar to their host came through the doors, their arms laden with silver platters and bowls. The five were served potato and garlic soup, chicken supreme, wild mushroom fricassee, saffron and leek coulis, figs roasted in honey and pistachios, with crème fraiche sorbet and honeycomb.

"You have been somewhat patient since you arrived, so please, eat and make yourself comfortable as I explain why you are all here. First of all, I am your host." He paused and saw only curious glances as the five people on the opposite side of the table began to eat. "I am the reason you're here."

"Hey mister, I'm not sure what to call most of this stuff," Doug said, "but it's pretty good."

"I'm so very happy you are enjoying it. I sometimes forget that the, ah, time difference between here and where you came from generally catches up with people at this point. So please, eat your fill. I have a feeling you'll be needing all of your energy soon."

The group continued to eat, speaking very little. They concentrated on their food and little else. As the platters and bowls were emptied, servers came and replenished everything until the five finally pushed their plates away and sat back. Then the servers came to clear away the dishes. A moment later they returned with fruit and cheese trays, plates of petit fours, slices of pound cake on silver trays, and hot coffee served in exclusive Bernardaud A La Reine coffee cups.

"My compliments to the chef," Benny said. "That spread was almost as good as the Sunday spread at Antonio's back in Jersey."

"Agreed. It was good. But all that aside," Tiffany said, "there is still the issue of why we're here. From what we have gathered, we are all here for different reasons. And the circumstances don't make sense."

"Oh, but the circumstances make perfect sense. You are just too self-absorbed to see it."

"Now see here—" Stewart Barton stood up.

"No, *you* see here." The host cut him off before he could finish. His eyes flashed and in that instant there was no trace of the moderately genial host he had been previously. "You were all so very concerned about your circumstances, but you never bothered to really look around you. You glossed over the landscape. You looked at the artwork and the books with only a passing curiosity. You were concerned with the potential reward for coming here, but not where *here* might be. No, none of that mattered." He stepped back, extended his left arm, and made a panoramic gesture with his hand.

"Then when you came into this room with the promise of the revelation you so badly wanted, you promptly went from various forms of righteous indignation and what little curiosity a few of you had, to gluttony. Pulling in to your own private world with no thought of how you might be connected to the other people in the same situation. Never asking the obvious questions, although Carol did touch on something briefly just a moment ago." He pointed to the mirror. "Just look at yourselves." The five watched and saw themselves as they had been earlier. Bent over their plates eating, paying no attention to their neighbors or anything else.

"What the hell?" Benny stood up. "Have you been recording us?"

"Not recording," their host said. "This mirror retains the history of everyone destined to reside in this place."

"Reside? I just came here for a business deal," Tiffany said, "I'm not planning to move in."

"Miss Thorne, why don't you just watch and let the reality of the situation play out. For example, if you'll turn your attention to the mirror, I think you'll be amazed at what the truth actually looks like."

As if a camera had panned downward, the five watched as the scene shifted and the contents of their plates were revealed. The potato and garlic soup was covered in mold. Maggots writhed and burrowed into the chicken supreme. The wild mushroom fricassee was covered in a blackish gelatinous film, and the saffron and leek coulis, figs roasted in honey, and pistachios with crème fraiche sorbet and honeycomb was obviously rancid. Black bugs skittered over the desert. When the figs were cut, they ruptured, and a greenish-gray mass like a malignant tumor rolled onto the plates.

Carol was the first to throw up. The others followed suit in quick succession. Doug began to cry and Tiffany screamed that it must be a trick, and she was going to sue whoever was responsible.

"*No!*" Stewart Burton screamed and pointed to the fruit bowls on the table.

The remaining fruit was rotten. The petit fours which were left were cracked and shriveled, and smelled like a long infected sore. The cake was greenish-black and covered with flies.

The five, physically and emotionally wrung out by the experience, sagged back in their chairs; pale, wide-eyed, and horrified. The silence was eventually broken by Carol who continued to retch.

"Ladies and gentlemen," their host said, "I brought you all here under false pretenses. In short, I lied." He stopped to let his words sink in. "And thanks to your guilt and greed, it was really very easy. So, let us start over, beginning with the introductions.

"My name is Baal. I am your host." He grinned as the lights lowered.

"Welcome to hell."

•

Benny was the first to regain some semblance of his composure.

"I don't know what kind of sick game you're playing here you freak, but I'm done. I'm getting out of here and if any of the rest of you have a brain in your head, you'll come with me." He grabbed a knife from the table and pointed it at Baal while he made his way to the door. "And you'd better keep your distance. Believe me, I will use this."

Baal made a small bow and gestured toward the door. "Please, go ahead."

Benny grabbed the ornate door handle, twisted it, and opened the door to reveal a solid brick wall. He turned to the group, his face slack. "What the..."

Baal walked over and closed the door. "Mr. Taglio, you just don't understand, do you?" He opened the door again and the library was visible, just as it had been when they came in. He closed it again. "You cannot leave. You will *never* be able to leave. You have made your proverbial bed, and now you are going to lie in it."

He took the knife from Benny and held it up for the other four to see. The metal melted and ran like water over his hand. "Go sit down and pay attention. We'll start with your story. And the rest of you," he said and pointed to the mirror, "watch and learn."

The mirror swirled, brightened, and the swirls resolved into a scene involving Benny and a man they didn't know. They appeared to be in a warehouse.

The man was strapped to a chair. His legs and arms were strapped down and there was a strip of duct tape across his mouth. The chair was bolted to the floor.

It stood in the middle of a dark stain.

A single bulb suspended from the ceiling cast shadows on the obviously terrified man.

"After everything I have done for you." The Benny in the mirror shook his head and walked to a nearby table. He ran his finger along the table top, two inches of solid oak. "After giving you a job. After seeing to it you could provide for your family in a style you'd never have been able to do on your own." He spat the words as if they left a foul taste in his mouth.

Benny walked along the table, looking at an array of tools. Drill. Pipe wrench. Long handled screw driver. Hacksaw. Bolt cutters. Carpet knife. He stopped.

Picked up a hammer.

"And how do you repay my generosity?" He slammed the hammer down on the table. The other tools bounced and skittered. The hammer head left a half inch divot in the scarred table top.

Benny turned and took a step toward the man, the hammer gripped in his left hand, his knuckles white.

"You stole from me." He took another step. The man in the chair whipped his head from side to side, the muffled sound coming from his sealed lips sounding like *oh, oh, I int. oh, I int.*

Benny walked up to the man, leaned in close. "You stole from *ME*," he screamed and swung the hammer. The man's left knee made a wet crunching sound and a dark stain spread across his lap. He rocked from side to side and did his best to scream through the duct tape. But Benny was like a man possessed. Alternately screaming, "*Nobody steals from me, you ungrateful bastard,*" and swinging the hammer harder and faster.

"*Nobody!*"

The man's other knee exploded. Though strapped to the chair, his jerking with each blow was growing more frantic. The chair strained against the bolts that held it to the floor.

Stewart Burton was mumbling "*no, no, no,*" while Doug yelled, "*Son of a bitch!*" and vomited. Tiffany Thorne closed her eyes and moaned.

Baal put his lips near her ear. "Watch the mirror or I'll cut your eyelids off and you won't have any choice."

In the mirror, the man continued to jerk and writhe, bones breaking, an eye now missing, the ruined optic nerve plastered to his cheek, teeth shattered, his screams mostly absorbed by the now bloody duct tape until five minutes later when Benny brought the hammer down on the top of the man's head. There was a wet thwack, like an overripe cantaloupe hitting the curb, and the man's struggles stopped. Benny walked away, the hammer stuck fast in place.

Carol retched again. Tiffany looked around the table, her now white complexion a stark contrast to her red dress. No one spoke for a long moment.

"I don't know where you got that," Benny said, his fists clenched, "but a man has the right to protect his business, and I was—"

"Please just shut up," Baal said, his black eyes flashing. "I for one don't care about your little temper tantrum with Marvin Plummer."

Benny's eyes bugged. He opened his mouth to speak, but Baal waved him down. "Yes, I know Marvin Plummer was your accountant and I know you think you caught him stealing from you—"

"Now you wait just a damn minute," Benny said, his voice low. "I know for a fact that he—"

One second Baal was beside the mirror, and the next, he was beside Benny leaning in hard. "You interrupt me one more time you little Italian *stronzo*, and I will rip your tongue out and feed it back to you right here and now. Do you understand me?" He didn't wait for an answer. Just wheeled around and walked back to the mirror. He pointed to what used to be Marvin Plummer.

"Benny 'The Hammer' Taglio. You can all see how he came by his nick-name. Benny made his bones by alternately coercing cooperation from and permanently ending the lives of dozens of people just like Mister Plummer with little more than duct tape and a hammer. And now that he is the top man in his particular little family, he still prefers to take matters into his own hands from time to time." He looked at the group around the table. They had all moved down so that Benny was sitting by himself. Still, no one spoke. They just stared at the spectacle playing out before them.

"Again, I don't particularly care," Baal said as he looked toward the ceiling and rolled his eyes, "but there are rules, not of my making. And the rules have to do with the innocents. You see, Benny," Baal gestured toward the corpse in the mirror, "your accountant also felt that someone was stealing from you. And because of how good you had been to him, and because you had made it possible for him to take care of his family in high style, and because he was the most loyal member of your little family, he was investigating on his own. And he was successful. He found the person who was really stealing from you.

"Johnny Fontana."

"What the…oh, sorry." Benny sat back in his chair, his eyes wide.

Baal chuckled. "You were going to say that Johnny Fontana was the one who told you that Marvin was skimming and even told you that he had found some of the money in the accountant's desk. Then he handed you a stack of bills and you went batshit crazy. You told Johnny to take him out to the warehouse and get him ready."

Benny nodded but said nothing.

"But what you didn't do was think things through. You didn't ask yourself why there was a stack of bills in his desk just two doors down from your office, if they were indeed stolen. You didn't ask him to explain himself. And you didn't ask yourself how a moron like Johnny could have uncovered a scheme like this since he was too stupid to do more than pick up money and bring it to Marvin."

Understanding dawned hard and Benny blanched. Baal walked over and leaned down until he was eye level with Benny.

"So, Benny 'The Hammer' Taglio killed an innocent man because he was too mad, too greedy, and too stupid to check out the story. And the remote land you thought you were picking up for a song, the land that would soon be full of people who disappeared, doesn't exist. But you were too greedy to check out that story too. And here you are."

Benny stared at Baal, his face slack.

"Well that's fine for him, but why are the rest of us here? We're not mob bosses and petty criminals." Carol tried to sound tough, but she still kept stealing worried glances at the mirror.

"No, you're not a petty criminal," Baal said as he moved closer. Carol shrank back in her chair, trying to maximize the distance between them. Baal leaned down and put his head next to hers, forcing them both to watch the mirror, cheek to cheek. "There is nothing petty about this at all."

The mirror seemed to distort and flex, then the group was watching Carol fix breakfast for a man in a wheelchair. She made oatmeal, raisin toast, and bacon while the dark-haired man sat at the breakfast table and looked on, his face bright.

"Tell me, did he taste the Aconite? That's some nasty stuff. It's actually a form of wolf's bane. Did you know that? It causes diarrhea and vomiting followed by an irregular heartbeat and numbness in the limbs. The victim actually dies from heart and respiratory system paralysis. It is indeed a horrible death. And it's almost impossible to detect. But I guess you knew that because you researched it for a week on that tablet you bought at a pawn shop. Then you smashed it and threw it in the river."

In the mirror, the man at the table was clutching his chest and vomiting. Carol was standing behind him, out of the way. She tapped her finger on her cellphone and shook her head. "Ben, it wouldn't have been as bad if you hadn't cheated on me with my best friend."

The man shook his head and gestured wildly at the cellphone. Carol slipped it in her pocket.

"Oh don't worry. I'll call 919, but not just yet. I have to make sure it has been long enough that the poison doesn't show up in your system. I figure about another forty-five minutes should do it..."

"You thought he was putting it to your best friend. But that's not really the case, Carol."

She pushed away from him, her eyes blazing. "Oh really? Then tell me why he was seen by two different friends of ours at a hotel with my friend

Beth. They were in the hotel restaurant having dinner when he was supposed to be at a conference."

"Well that's simple," Baal said, his black eyes gleaming. "Beth's cousin, her favorite cousin, is the manager of the hotel and she was helping him plan your fifteenth wedding anniversary party there. He was getting a sweet deal on rooms for some of your friends and tickets for everybody to a Broadway show touring in the area that weekend. One you've wanted to see for years. And he had just set everything up and was buying Beth dinner as a way of thanking her for making it all possible. And you know the last thing he told her when she was on her way out and he was staying for one last cup of coffee. Here, watch this."

The mirror seemed to flash, and then there was her husband and Beth. He hugged Carol's friend, a very platonic hug between friends, and said, "I will never be able to adequately thank you and your cousin. Hell, he's *my* favorite cousin now." They both laughed, and he waved a waiter over and asked for more coffee. "I just hope this weekend gives her some inkling of how much I love her."

The scene froze.

Carol's face blanched.

"And because you didn't even ask either of them about what was happening, just assumed they were up to no good, you killed an innocent man. And again, while I don't care one way or the other," he rolled his eyes toward the ceiling again and grimaced, "rules are rules."

Stewart Burton cleared his throat, his attention primarily directed toward the mirror. "Are we, then, to understand that we have all in one way or another found ourselves in the same situation as Benny and Carol? Why go through this charade if we are all condemned to hell? Why not take us when we die instead of duping us and bringing us here under false pretenses?"

"Mister Stewart Burton the third, the answer is simple." Baal smiled and spread his arms out wide. "I did it because it's fun."

•

He regarded the suited man for a moment, then his grin widened. “You know your little bit of handiwork might just be the most impressive of all, because you weren’t in the room with your victim when he died. You weren’t even in the state. No sir, you had some lovely doctored pictures of Frederick Payne in bed with a male hooker. They were really quite good. And quite explicit. And the really funny thing is, he was as straight as an arrow and had never even considered visiting a hooker of any kind. Then when you sent him the photographs anonymously and said they would be released if he did not resign from the board of Dexter, Davis, and Feldman, he was so scared, even though he knew no such thing had ever happened, that he hanged himself.”

Here the mirror swirled and cleared, to show a man bucking and jerking at the end of a length of nylon cord. He appeared to be in a parking garage.

“Bravo, mister Burton. You really rattled him with that one. But it did get him off the board, and with you as the most likely candidate to fill the next board position, it worked out really well for you. Still, while you had already decided that the day he resigned you would delete everything and destroy the laptop you were using, he didn’t know that. No, Mr. Frederick Payne, recently of Palm Springs, figured anyone who would go to such lengths would just keep going and would probably release the phony photos anyway. He figured he would be on the hook for the rest of his life.

“So, he waited until everyone was gone for the day and went to a remote corner of the parking deck to do the deed. He knew he had time. He knew with it being Friday that no one would be back before Monday. And he knew this way the manufactured scandal had the least chance of affecting his family and friends.

“But what he didn’t know about was the slight give of the nylon rope, so it took him twenty-two minutes to die. His neck didn’t break. He strangled to death. And his feet were within three inches of the floor the whole time. So close, yet so far away.” He gestured toward the mirror. “Look how he struggled. Such a horrible way to go, although I do love that shade of purple they turn.”

Stewart Burton stared at Baal, then watched the mirror, his face slack and pale. After a moment he turned to look at his companions at the table. Every one of them had a similar expression. Numb horror and resignation.

"OK folks, enough of this. Our final two events of the evening should prove to be just as interesting as the ones we have seen so far. But in the interest of time, because your journey is just beginning, let's take a look simultaneously."

The mirror began to smoke and flash. Then, as if in split screen, two scenes dissolved into place. In one, Tiffany was in the arms of a man in what appeared to be a hallway under construction. As the embrace became more heated, she steered him toward a nearby wall.

He moved with her willingly.

In a movement that obviously took him by surprise, Tiffany stopped suddenly and shoved her companion sideways through what at first looked like an open doorway. She walked to the edge of the opening, actually an open elevator, and looked down.

Her unlucky companion was at the bottom of the elevator shaft, thirteen floors down, twitching on an exposed length of rebar sticking up out of the floor. She continued to watch him until the twitching stopped, then looked around and saw a hammer near a pile of construction materials. She removed a glove from her pocket, picked up the hammer, and dropped it thirteen floors where it landed on the man's shoulder and bounced off. She heard the bone crack, but the man remained motionless.

Tiffany put the glove in her pocket and hummed a popular tune as she walked down the hallway.

On the opposite side of the mirror, Doug was standing over a figure lying on a piece of plywood resting on two saw horses. They appeared to be in a barn.

"No, oh hell no. We're not doing this."

Baal turned and saw Doug standing at his place at the table. He was shaking and the front of his shirt was stained from vomit he had wiped off earlier. His or someone else's. He was pointing toward the mirror and making his way around the table.

"Mister Bumpass, sit down."

Doug stopped, but continued to point at the mirror. "Hey, I never told you my last name."

"And yet, I still know it. Now sit down while you still can."

Doug took another step, "Hell no, we ain't doing this. This ain't none of your damn business."

One second Doug was ranting and pointing at the mirror, and the next, Baal was in front of him, gripping his right index and ring fingers in his fists.

"Mister Bumpass," he said, and snapped Doug's fingers to opposite sides with an audible crack, "go sit down."

Doug howled in pain, his face a mask of agony. When he finally caught his breath he screamed, "You broke my damn fingers you stupid mother—"

Baal took Doug's head in his hands. Fine wisps of smoke rose between his fingers. "Finish that sentence," he said, his eyes blazing. "I dare you."

Doug screamed. "*Stop. That burns. Stop…stop…please stop.*" The smell of singed hair and flesh filled the room as did his sobs of pain.

Baal continued to hold his head and pulled him in close, as the burning smell faded. "Boy, you are in a world of hurt right now, but I can't believe you're so stupid as to think that things can't get any worse." He shoved Doug away and walked back to his original spot. "Because I can assure you, they can. So, you would do well to keep a civil tongue in your head."

Doug did not respond. He rested his mangled hand in his lap and touched his head gingerly. The effort made him gasp.

"Now, as I was saying," Baal said. .ome of his control had returned, though he still eyed Doug, "Mister Bumpass was about to demonstrate why he has come to be in your company." He flicked a finger and the frozen image on the screen began to move again. Doug spoke to the woman on the make-shift table, though she appeared to be unconscious.

"I ain't going down because you're too good to help me out of a jam. No ma'am. Mister Barnwell said to deal with you, and that's exactly what I'm going to do. Then I'm going to let Joe watch me dispose of your sorry ass."

The picture seemed to widen, and a third figure was visible sitting in a chair in a far corner of the barn. He nodded for Doug to continue.

Doug picked up an axe and began to hack the girl on the table to pieces. When the process bogged down, he used a hacksaw. After what seemed like hours, the figure in the chair spoke up.

"OK, that should be enough. Now go get those contractor bags, the buckets, and the cement. It's going to be a long night."

The picture froze and Baal addressed the group.

"Miss Thorne just dealt with the man whom she believed was the stumbling block on her ascent up the corporate ladder in the Las Vegas casino where she works. She was on the list for promotion, but so was the recently deceased Randall Thomas. Every time she wanted to discuss the promotion with him, get this opinion on what was taking the casino heads so long to make the decision, he became evasive or just walked away altogether. And all the bosses would say is that there were ongoing discussions.

"But nobody was discussing anything with her. And that made her suspicious. The bosses must have been talking with Randall and not her. Isn't that right, Miss Thorne?"

Tiffany opened her mouth to say something, glanced at Doug who was still moaning and holding his head, and said nothing.

"Oh Miss Thorne, you made up so many scenarios in your head. You just knew it was a matter of the good old boys' network at work again, and you didn't stand a chance. But here's what you didn't know." Baal smiled and showed off two rows of sharp, white teeth. "Randall Thomas had a family."

Tiffany looked up, a look of surprise on her face. "I…he…he never said." Her face went pale, her eyes wide.

"Oh yes. And he had the opportunity to become casino manager with one of the other casinos on the strip. But negotiations were at a critical stage, and he couldn't afford for word to leak out. So, he played his cards close to the vest, so to speak. He didn't ask to have his name removed from the promotion because that would raise some questions he wasn't prepared to answer yet. And he couldn't confide in you because you had never given him any reason to trust you.

"So, you asked him to meet you in the section of the casino that was being renovated. And when you came on to him, he was surprised, but he is still only human. For a brief moment he let the scene play out. And just as he was having second thoughts, you pushed him through the open elevator shaft. Knowing full well that there were no working cameras in that section and it would be the next morning before anyone went up there to resume work.

"Another thing you didn't know," Baal said as he put his hands on the table and leaned over in front of Tiffany, "is that the job was yours. The other casino was going to offer him the job and you would get your promotion." He slammed one hand down on the table, leaving a smoking handprint. Tiffany began to cry, her breath hitching and the ragged sobs echoing off the mahogany walls. "Oh yes, there is one more thing you didn't know," Baal said and smiled. "It took him another twenty minutes to die after you dropped the hammer down the shaft. And he was in agony the whole time.

"Now, to the final case of the evening. Our friend Doug here had borrowed money he couldn't pay back," Baal said and made a *tisk tisk* sound. "He wanted to borrow enough to purchase drugs. A lot of drugs. Our friend Doug here had in mind to become something of a drug tycoon. The only problem is: Doug is not too bright."

Doug looked up, a scowl on his face, but he didn't speak.

"No, he is so stupid that he was cheated when he went to make the transaction. He went alone, figuring that they would just give him the drugs as soon as he handed over the briefcase with the money in it. Just like trading baseball cards or buying a crap at a yard sale from a neighbor.

"But what happened? Doug took seventy thousand dollars to an empty industrial park, four guys got out of a Lincoln town car, asked to see the money, and he handed them the briefcase. Three of them got in the car while the driver watched to see what Doug would do. When Doug walked over, all cool, and sat on the hood of his car, the driver shot out two of Doug's tires, got in the car, and drove off."

Baal and Doug's four companions looked at the bargain basement drug kingpin. Doug just sniffed and tried to find a position that didn't cause his broken fingers to make him want to cry.

Baal shook is head. "The next day when he went to see his benefactor, instead of being greeted with charity and understanding, Doug was told he had twenty-four hours to repay the money. Doug pleaded for more time, but the benefactor, a mister Bud Ellis, was firm. Twenty-four hours, or he would end up on a missing person's list."

"Boy, you are one big *idiota*," Benny said. "*Non riesco a credere a quando sei stupido,*" he said, then remembered his situation. "I'm sorry—"

"Not at all," Baal said, showing his pointed teeth in a smile. "I can't believe how stupid he is either." He turned his attention back to the group. "When Bud Ellis said he must have something worth twenty-five thousand, maybe his car, the ever-chivalrous Doug said, 'I couldn't sell that. My girl loves that car." Doug's head jerked up at what sounded like his own voice coming from the ugly little man.

"Then, Mr. Ellis gave him a way out. He said if Doug delivered his girl to a certain house in the mountains for the weekend, all would be forgiven. They would be square."

"Don't tell me the dumb ass considered it," Carol said, the disgust in her voice obvious. There was murmuring around the table, spurred on by Doug's situation, as if the group had forgotten their own plight.

"Oh, it gets better," Baal said. "Doug left there and went to find his girl, Clara. When he explained the situation to her, she screamed at him and threw him out of her house with the admonition to never come back again.

"You see, the thing about Clara was, she had only known Doug for a couple of months, and in that time, he had never even gotten to second base, if you know what I mean."

"She said she was saving herself for marriage," Doug said, then screamed as Tiffany smacked his hand. "Hey bitch, I was in trouble," he said as the tears of pain flowed down his cheeks.

"You still are," Baal said, not smiling. "But you called Bud Ellis and told him she refused. After a minute or two, he gave you a way out again. And what did he ask you to do?"

Doug looked at his mangled hand and wouldn't look up.

"Let me help you remember," Baal said as his voice took on a thick southern accent. "You bring me her head in a bag tomorrow, dispose of the rest, and then don't ever come around me again."

Doug's breath came in ragged gasps and all he could do was shake his head.

Baal crossed his arms over his chest and shook his head. "They made it really easy. A little chloroform, a ride out to an abandoned barn, and all you had to do was follow through on the request from a low-level country loan shark. And from what we saw earlier, you didn't hesitate. You killed and dismembered an innocent young woman to save your own hide. And all you really had to do was sell the damn car."

The atmosphere in the room changed; the images in the mirror swirled and dissipated like smoke, then only the room was reflected again. And the room was becoming warmer .

At some point during the exchanges, the servers had cleared away the table; only the stained table cloth remained. Servers had taken up positions behind each of the five occupied chairs.

"And that, ladies and gentlemen, brings us to the crux of the matter. To the reason you are here. Now that your last meal is over—"as Baal said this, Carol retched violently—"it is time for your just desserts so to speak. Please stand up and turn around."

As they turned, the servers each took a sideways step so their view would be clear. Gone were the mahogany walls, the curtains, the brass fixtures. Now they were facing a long white hallway at the end of which was a blank wall.

"What?" Stewart Burton turned back to Baal, the shock evident on his face. "How? What is happening here?" he said when he turned to face their host.

The others turned and Tiffany said, "Where is the table? Where's the room?"

There was no table. No paneled walls. No sign a meal had been served or could have been served. There was no mirror on the wall. Just the wall on their end of the long white hallway.

"Oh, my good Lord in Heaven," Benny said as the color drained from his face.

Baal winced, then smiled. "I'm afraid it's much too late for that. Your 'good Lord in Heaven' does not come to this place. Did you not believe me when I said 'Welcome to Hell?' It was not hyperbole."

Doug, still cradling his hand, shook his head. "Oh no. I don't know where we are, but this ain't hell. I went to Sunday school and this ain't what they told us it would be like. So, you tell us right now where we are."

"Look, the boy isn't all that bright," Tiffany said, her face pale, but her voice somewhat stronger than it had been, "but he's got a point. This doesn't look much like hell. And everything you've done could be accomplished with special effects. So—"

Baal held out his arm and made a squeezing gesture with his hand. As his fist started to close, Tiffany's face went scarlet and her eyes widened. She began to gag and gasp. Baal lifted his arm and Tiffany's feet left the ground. The others screamed and started to run, but they were caught and returned to their places by the servers. Just before she passed out, Baal released his grip and Tiffany fell to the floor. She held her throat, still making choking sounds.

There were bruises and red finger marks on her throat.

No one moved to help her.

"How was that for a special effect? Anybody else want a taste?"

The others backed up as far as the servants allowed.

"I didn't think so. So come, walk with me." Baal headed down the long white hallway. "Yes, there is the lake of fire and all that Sunday school stuff. And yes, they beg and plead and scream for mercy. But this," he waved toward the end of the hall, "is reserved for the special cases. Not just run of the mill sinners, but those who kill innocents." He stopped at the end of the hall and turned to face the five. "People like you."

"But there's nothing here," Carol said. "Just a long hallway. I didn't even see any doors. So if this is hell, will we just wander around for eternity being bored silly?"

"You know what amazes me?" Baal asked. "There is something about this present generation that is unlike anything I've ever seen in all the time I've been here." He shook his head and let out a deep sigh. The room suddenly stank of carrion and spoiled milk. "It's the arrogance. Even the Nazis who ran the concentration camps showed some sign of remorse by this point. And yes," he said, smiling a reptilian smile that didn't quite reach his eyes, "they are your neighbors here, though you won't ever meet them. You'll be too busy."

"Busy doing what," Benny asked.

Baal's eyes narrowed and the smile widened.

"Dying."

•

Five doors opened in the wall in front of them. Five doors where there had been no doors. It looked like five massive pocket doors sliding into the wall itself. The rooms beyond were white.

Empty.

"Welcome to your home for eternity. And before you ask, Benny, no it's not going to be like solitary confinement. No sitting here for all eternity as the walking dead. Oh no. Not for you five.

"As I have said, and you have all seen, you are here because you have killed an innocent. And as the character Andre Linoge said in Stephen King's insightful work, *Storm of the Century*, 'hell is repetition.' And you are about to see just how right he was. Because each of you is going to die in exactly the same way you killed your victims. For example, Benny, you will be beaten to death with a hammer the same way you killed Marvin Plummer." Baal gestured toward the room behind Benny, and when he turned around, the room was no longer empty. There was an abandoned warehouse with a display of tools on a table, and a chair bolted to the floor. An exact replica of the place he killed his victim.

"And for you Tiffany, behold." Baal gestured and her empty room was now a long hallway under construction with an open elevator door among the stacks of drywall, insulation, paint, hammers, and other building supplies. "It's an exact match. And this will be the case for all of you except for Stewart Burton's space. Yours is proving to be quite interesting."

By this point, each room had transformed into an exact replica of the scene of their individual crimes except for the room before Stewart Burton. His was still an empty white space. And before any of them could try to bolt for the other end of the hall, the servers grabbed them from behind and held them fast, forcing them to face their fate.

"This is how it works. You will each be killed in the manner in which you killed your victim. You will experience the fear and the agony they experienced. And after you die, you will no longer be dead. You will be very much alive. And you will go through it all over again. But to make things interesting, you will remember every delicious detail of your previous pain, agony, and death. Then you will be killed, resurrected, and get to do it all over again.

"Forever." Baal smiled a genuine smile of pleasure. "You are in what Alice Cooper so aptly refers to in his song, a bad place alone."

Baal looked at Doug and shook his head.

"Now Doug here dismembered an unconscious woman. But not to worry, my friend. We are nothing if not fair here." He reached down and squeezed Doug's mangled hand. Doug screamed as Baal moved in closer and whispered, "You'll be awake for the whole thing." He released the hand and turned his attention to Stewart Burton.

"Mister Burton, you have proved to be a most interesting case because we didn't talk about all of your transgressions against the innocent, did we?"

"Look, I don't know what you're talking about. I haven't—"

"Really Mister Burton, if it was up to me, I'd have shown *all* of it. But," he looked toward the ceiling and rolled his eyes, "there are rules. Do I need to remind you of the children?"

Stewart Burton's eyes went wide as his face went bone white.

"I see it's all coming back to you. And again, while I really don't care, rules are rules. And you must pay. So, here's the deal." He waved his hand and the empty room transformed. It became an abandoned warehouse with a display of tools on a table, and a chair bolted to the floor. Then a long hallway under construction with an open elevator door among the stacks of drywall, insulation, paint, hammers, and other building supplies. One by one the room became a replica of the other four rooms, plus the back corner of the parking garage where Frederick Payne died.

"You will get to experience all of them, in no particular order."

Stewart Burton began to scream. He tried to jerk away from the server who held him, but to no avail. He was held to the spot.

"Oh, and did I mention, between every death, you will experience what the children you defiled experienced, only you will go through the experience until you die. And again, you will remember every excruciating thing between sessions."

Baal nodded, and in the midst of the screams and pleading, the servers dragged their individual charges into the rooms, transforming into something other than human with each step. Baal watched as the wall seemed to "heal" itself, reverting to a smooth blank white wall.

Baal turned away from the wall and all was instantly transformed back into the dining room with its lush curtains and massive mirror. Baal smiled and went through the door leading into the library.

It was time for the first arrival of the next group.

Author's Note

The short story is a special breed of cat. Neil Gaiman once said, *"Short stories are tiny windows into other worlds and other minds and other dreams. They are journeys you can make to the far side of the universe and still be back in time for dinner."*

Also, short stories are a bit of an anomaly. It's possible to develop some facility in writing these shorter, self-contained "windows into other worlds…" over time, and turn out some fairly good work. But if you're dedicated, you can spend a lifetime learning to write short stories that have the potential to be something transformative.

Some that stand out for me include Ray Bradbury's "There Will Come Soft Rains." The story centers around the only house left standing after a nuclear holocaust. The automated systems are unaware that there is no one in the house and continue as normal. When a fire breaks out, the house is destroyed. When the flames have burned themselves out, the only sound that can be heard is a mechanical voice coming from the only standing wall, continually calling out the date and time.

Another one that stands out is Robert Arthur's story, "Obstinate Uncle Otis." I read this one in *Alfred Hitchcock's Ghostly Gallery: Eleven Spooky Stories for Young People* back in 1966. The story deals with an obstinate old man named Otis (hence the title) who was struck by lightning. But instead of being killed, he was given a strange power. If he said he didn't believe in something, it ceased to exist.

Immediately.

At one point in the story Otis falls, hits his head, and believes himself to be Eustace Lingam, a farm machinery salesman from Cleveland Ohio. He insists he has never heard of Otis Morks. A few nights later as his nephew and sister are sitting downstairs, they hear one shoe hit the floor, then they hear Otis say, "I don't believe there is any such person as Otis Morks." Then...only silence. When the nephew and his aunt go upstairs to check on him, there is an empty bed with one shoe on the floor.

Man, I loved that story.

Then there's Charles L. Grant, the master of what has come to be known as "Quiet Horror." He was the writer who really introduced me to the horror genre. I remember reading "Temperature Days on Hawthorne Street," "A Crowd of Shadows," "Hear Me Now, My Sweet Abbey Rose," and "If Damon Comes." Those four short stores have stayed with me since I first read them decades ago. Through a strange series of events, I not only met Charlie Grant, but he became my mentor, and more importantly, my friend for over 25 years. And one of the highest compliments I have ever received was the day he called me about a short story I had submitted to the *Gothic Ghosts* anthology he and Wendy Web were editing.

"Before we get started," he said, "I just want to say something about that first page. Damn, I wish I'd written that."

And while I floated on that statement for a long time, he followed it up with, "But, you need to get rid of about five pages of dialogue. These folks talk a lot. And get rid of the character that shows up on page three. He doesn't add anything to the story."

The thing is, I've always considered myself an average short story writer at best, so the fact that you're holding a collection of my stories in your hands right now (thank you) has me a bit floored. I see stories like Shirley Jackson's, "The Lottery"; Stephen King's, "The Man in the Black Suit"; M. R. James' "Oh, Whistle and I'll Come to You, Lad,"; and Robert McCammon's, "Night Crawlers," and I think *That, boys and girls, is how it's done.*

Do any of the stories in this collection rise to that level? I don't think so. But I believe there are a few gems in here. I am a child of the 60s and 70s, and my stories definitely have the vibe of that era. I'm not what you might call cutting edge. I'm just a guy sitting in an office full of movie monsters, guitars, toys, Christmas ornaments, books, magazines, whittling tools, baseball caps, a purple monkey, a container full of pens on my desk, and other important things, who likes to tell stories.

In these pages you'll meet a professor who gets the offer of a lifetime, but it comes with a hefty price. Then, there's the creation of a famous mad scientist who has made an important decision. One that will have lasting consequences. There's also a short piece about a family outing in the cemetery. 'Nuff said as the Marvel folks used to say. There's also an old-fashioned mystery that makes much of the power of snow. And the story of a dinner party for five that is one of the saddest things I've ever written. A story of choices made and consequences earned.

So, take my hand and come with me. I'll take you to some of these "other places."

Just you and me on a walk through a lot of different neighborhoods. You should be OK. But remember this: The sun is setting. And if you get lost, I can't guarantee I'll be the one holding your hand in the dark.

Thomas Smith
Surf City, NC
October 2023